LEARN TO DRAW

CURSED PRINCESS CLUB

Lambcat

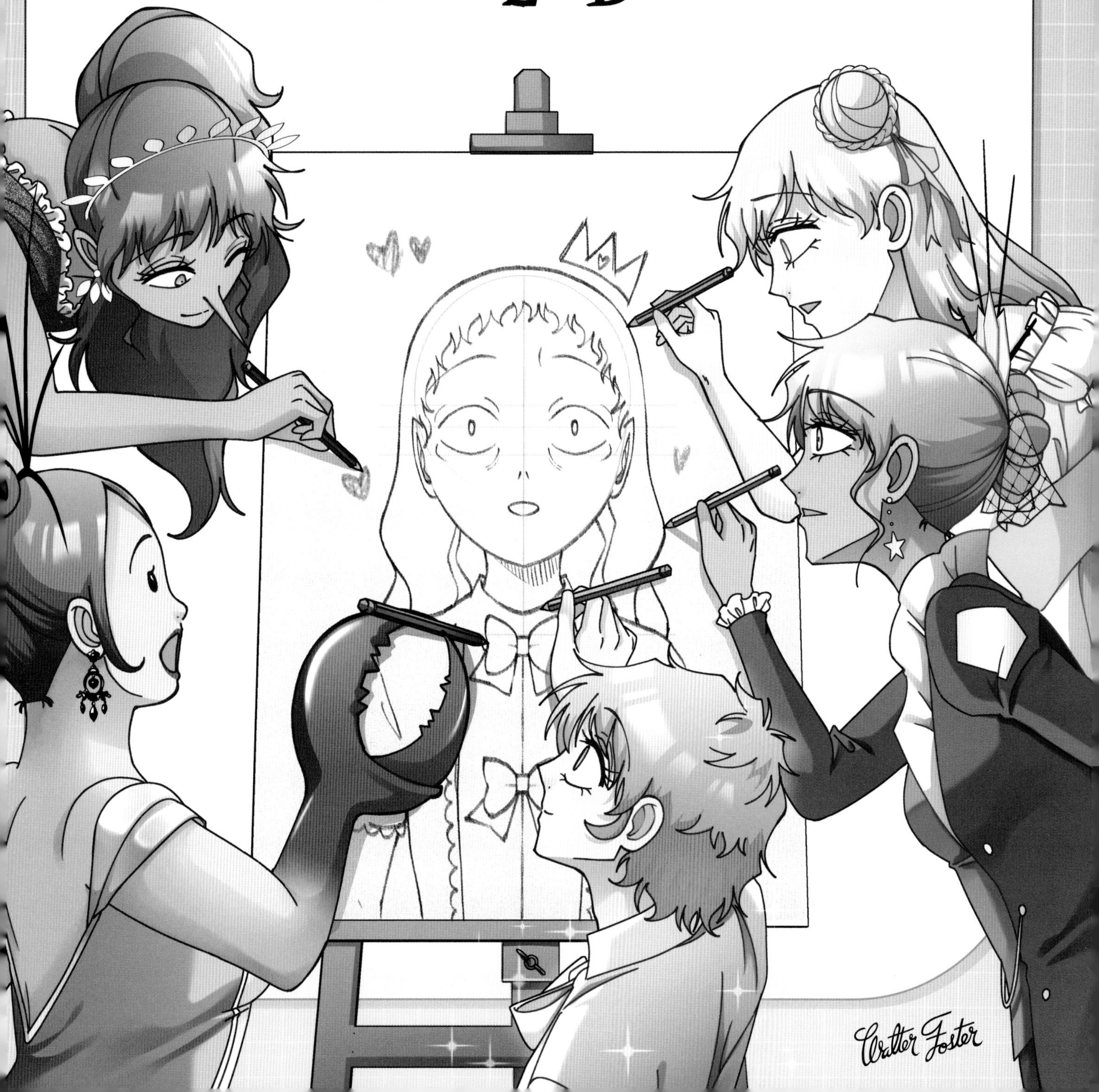

Walter Foster

Quarto.com | WalterFoster.com

© 2024 Quarto Publishing Group USA Inc.
Cursed Princess Club © Lambcat and WEBTOON Entertainment Inc. All rights reserved.
WEBTOON and all related trademarks are owned by WEBTOON Entertainment Inc. or its
affiliates.

First Published in 2024 by Walter Foster Publishing, an imprint of The Quarto Group,
100 Cummings Center, Suite 265-D, Beverly, MA 01915, USA.
T (978) 282-9590 F (978) 283-2742

Walter Foster Publishing titles are also available at discount for retail, wholesale, promotional,
and bulk purchase. For details, contact the Special Sales Manager by email at specialsales@
quarto.com or by mail at The Quarto Group, Attn: Special Sales Manager, 100 Cummings Center,
Suite 265-D, Beverly, MA 01915, USA.

10 9 8 7 6 5 4 3 2 1

ISBN: 978-0-7603-8973-7

Digital edition published in 2024
eISBN: 978-0-7603-8974-4

Library of Congress Cataloging-in-Publication Data is available.

Step-by-step artwork: Elizabeth T. Gilbert
Design, editorial, and layout: Coffee Cup Creative LLC
WEBTOON Rights and Licensing Manager: Amanda Chen
Illustrations and art: Lambcat and WEBTOON Entertainment,
     except Shutterstock on pages 34 and 35

Printed in USA

CONTENTS

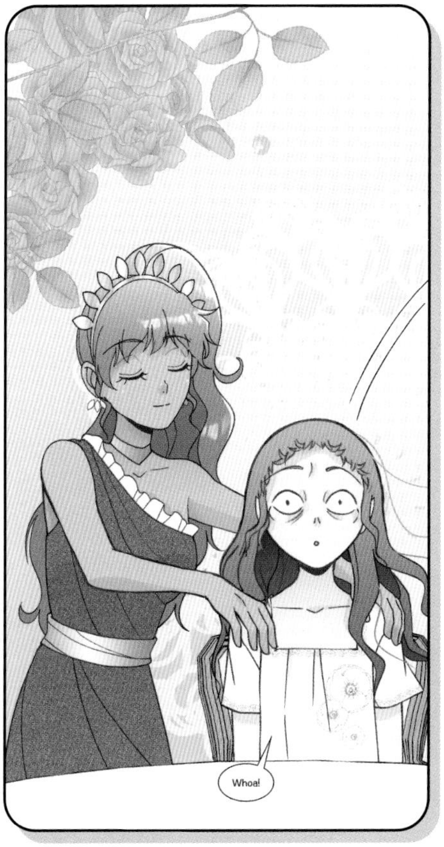
Whoa!

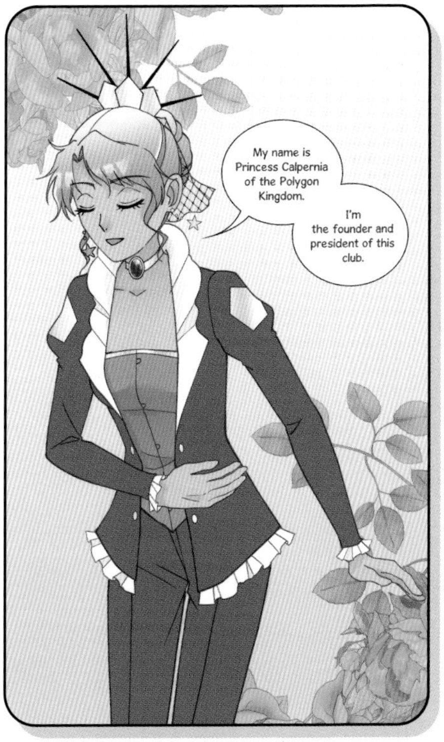
My name is Princess Calpernia of the Polygon Kingdom.
I'm the founder and president of this club.

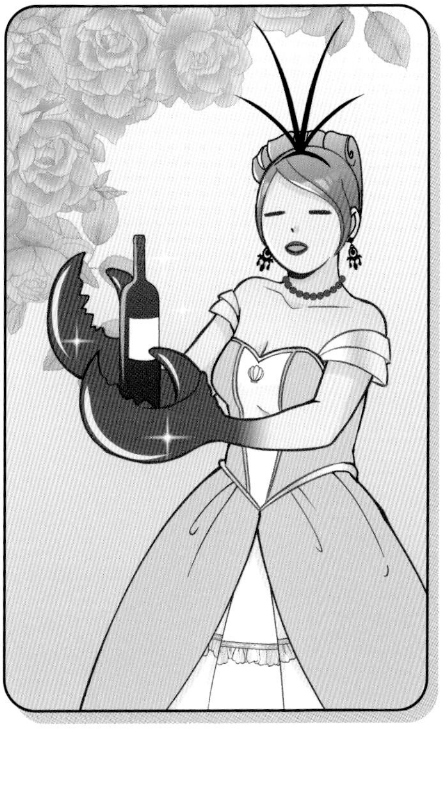

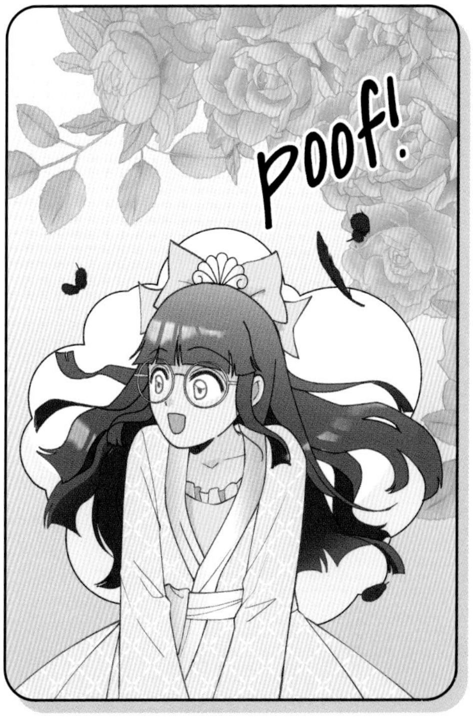
poof!

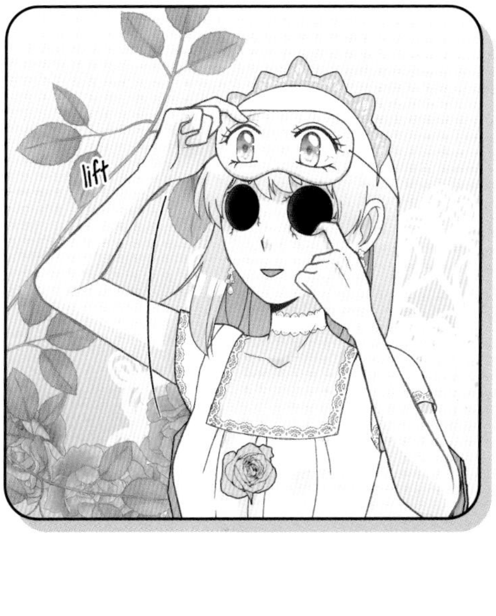
lift

INTRODUCTION

Just because you're cursed doesn't mean you're not special!

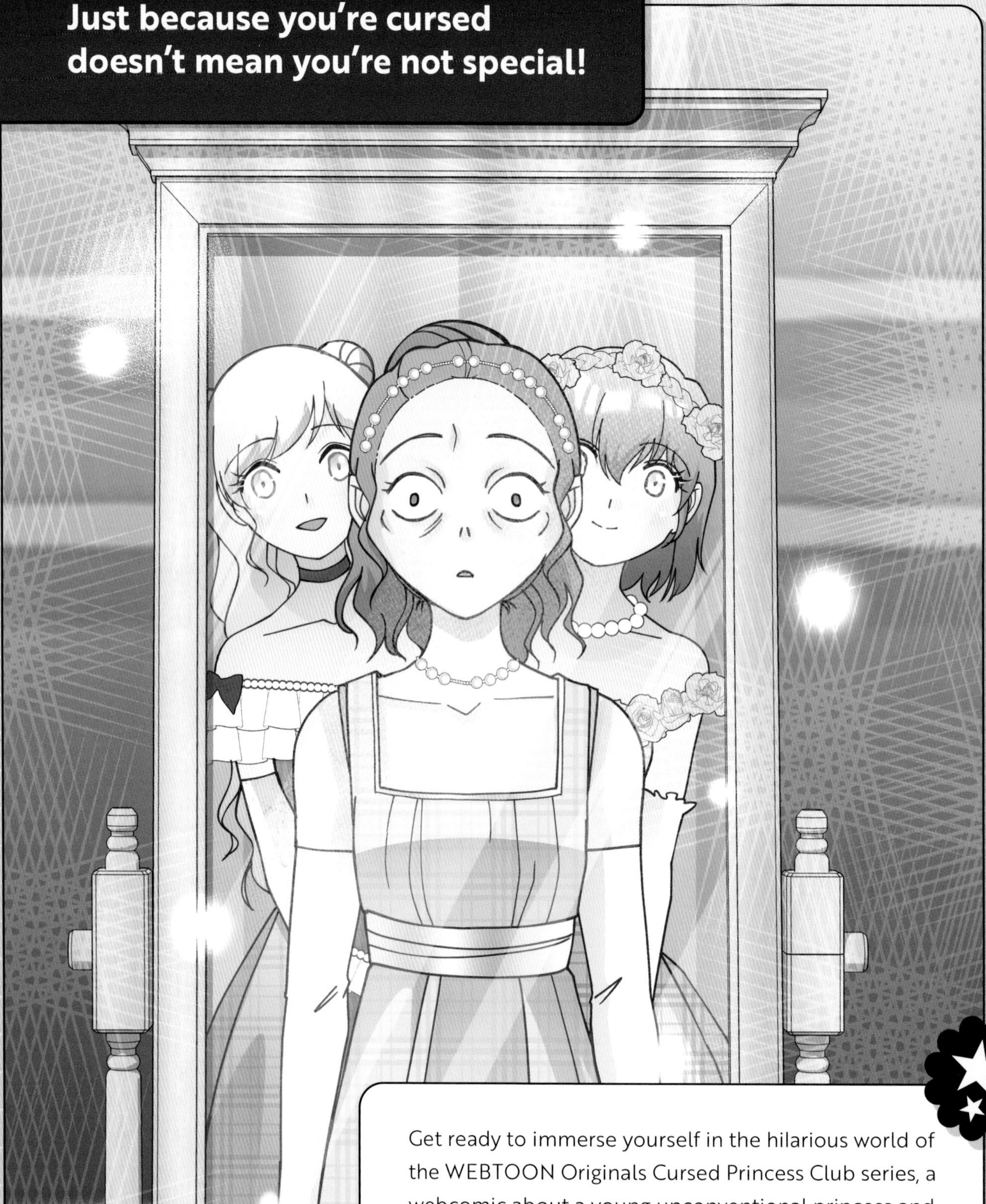

Get ready to immerse yourself in the hilarious world of the WEBTOON Originals Cursed Princess Club series, a webcomic about a young unconventional princess and her journey of self-exploration and how she stumbles upon a secret club she never knew she needed.

WHAT IS CURSED PRINCESS CLUB?

The Cursed Princess Club series follows the story of Gwendolyn, an unconventional fairy-tale princess who accidentally stumbles upon the twisted world of the Cursed Princess Club where she meets other princesses who have been hexed and cast out of their kingdoms. Gwendolyn is living proof that princesses don't always have it all!

Check out all the episodes of the hit WEBTOON series.

SYNOPSIS

The beautiful Pastel Kingdom is home to an equally beautiful royal family. Princess Lorena is so gorgeous that flowers bloom around her. Princess Maria is always surrounded by helpful woodland creatures. Prince Jamie is so radiant that he quite literally glows. And then there's Gwen. With her sickly green skin and her fanglike teeth, to say she doesn't quite fit the mold of her family would be an understatement.

Despite this, Gwen's family has always been loving and protective of her. It's not until the sisters are betrothed to princes from a neighboring kingdom that Gwen begins to understand just how different she really is. Thankfully, she's not without help. Gwen soon discovers the secret CPC—the Cursed Princess Club—a group of outcast royalty who might be exactly what she needs to learn that not fitting the mold doesn't make her any less of a princess.

WHAT IS A WEBCOMIC?

Webcomics are comics published on a website or mobile app.

Meet WEBTOON™.

We started a whole new way to create stories and opened it up to anyone with a story to tell. We're home to thousands of creator-owned series with amazing, diverse visions from all over the world. Get in on the latest original romance, comedy, action, fantasy, horror, and more from big names and big-names-to-be—made just for WEBTOON. We're available anywhere, anytime, and always for free.

FROM THE CREATOR

What was your inspiration behind creating your WEBTOON series?
I wanted to make a fairy-tale story, and one idea I stumbled upon was wondering what it would be like for characters in these worlds who don't get their happily-ever-afters. What about a princess that doesn't fit the mold of perfect beauty? And what parallels can that relate to in our own real-life experiences?

How did you get into creating your WEBTOON series?
Cursed Princess Club is my first attempt as a self-taught artist and author. I started it for a WEBTOON contest in 2018, and despite my incredibly bad art, WEBTOON was kind enough to give me the opportunity to launch my story. My background is in music, which I make in the form of soundtracks that accompany the webcomic.

Is there advice you would give your fans when trying to draw your characters or starting their own series?
The only piece of advice I feel qualified to give is: You don't have to wait until you're fully ready to begin drawing whatever it is you feel like drawing. And I hope seeing my incredibly rough early drawings for Cursed Princess Club is proof of that! I definitely feel like I learned to draw through making this comic, and I am still learning so much every day. One of the greatest ways to push yourself is to tell a story you wanna tell, whether it's through one drawing or an entire comic. So please don't let perfection stop you from starting!

This book may not teach you everything you need to know about drawing, as that is a lifelong journey (I am right there alongside you!). But I hope it provides some tips for anyone who needs inspiration, and that the step-by-step examples show that all the art you see is made up of simple shapes and lines. And by getting your arms, hands, and eyes used to them, I hope you feel comfortable exploring and continuing your drawing journey!

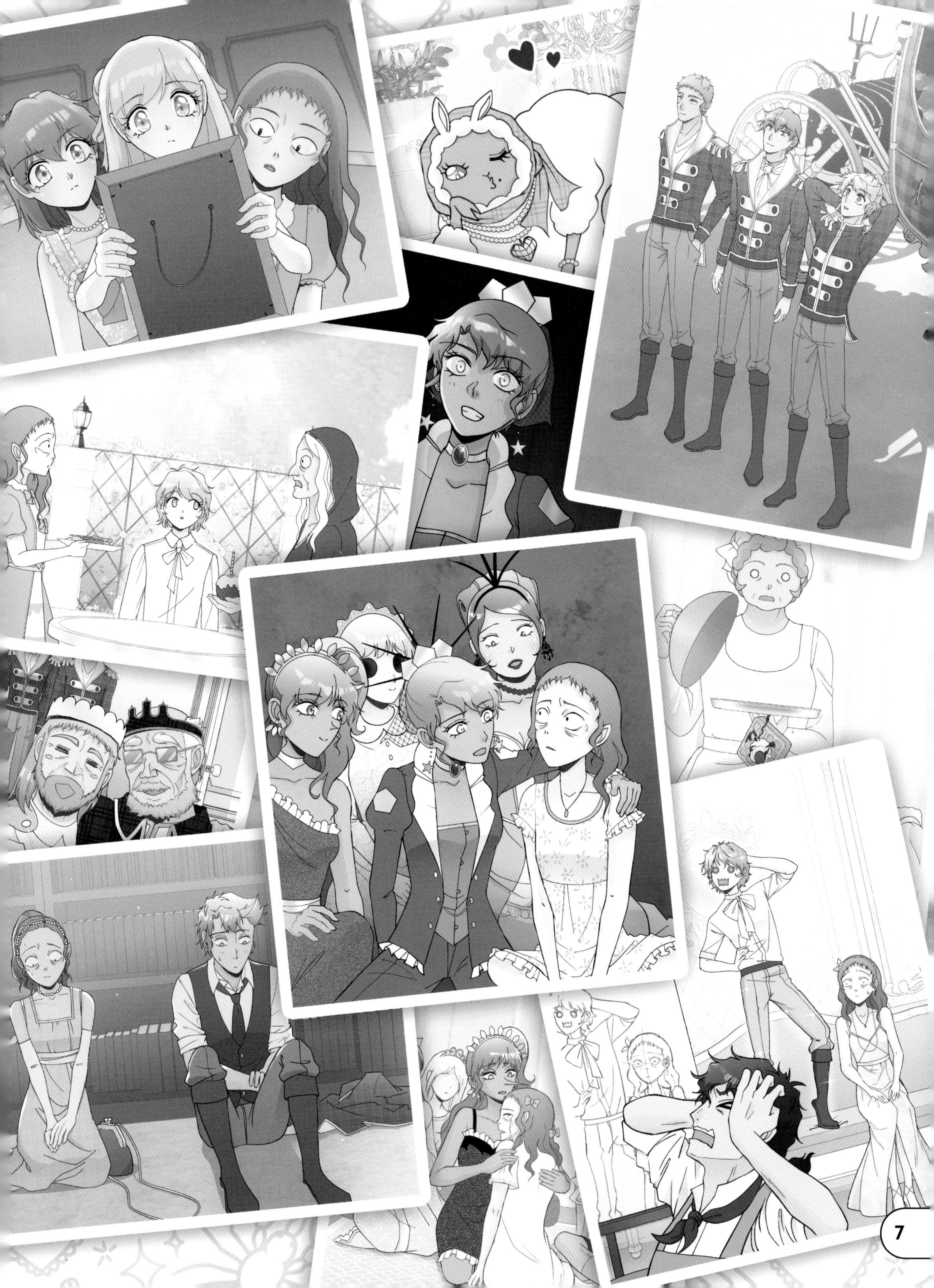

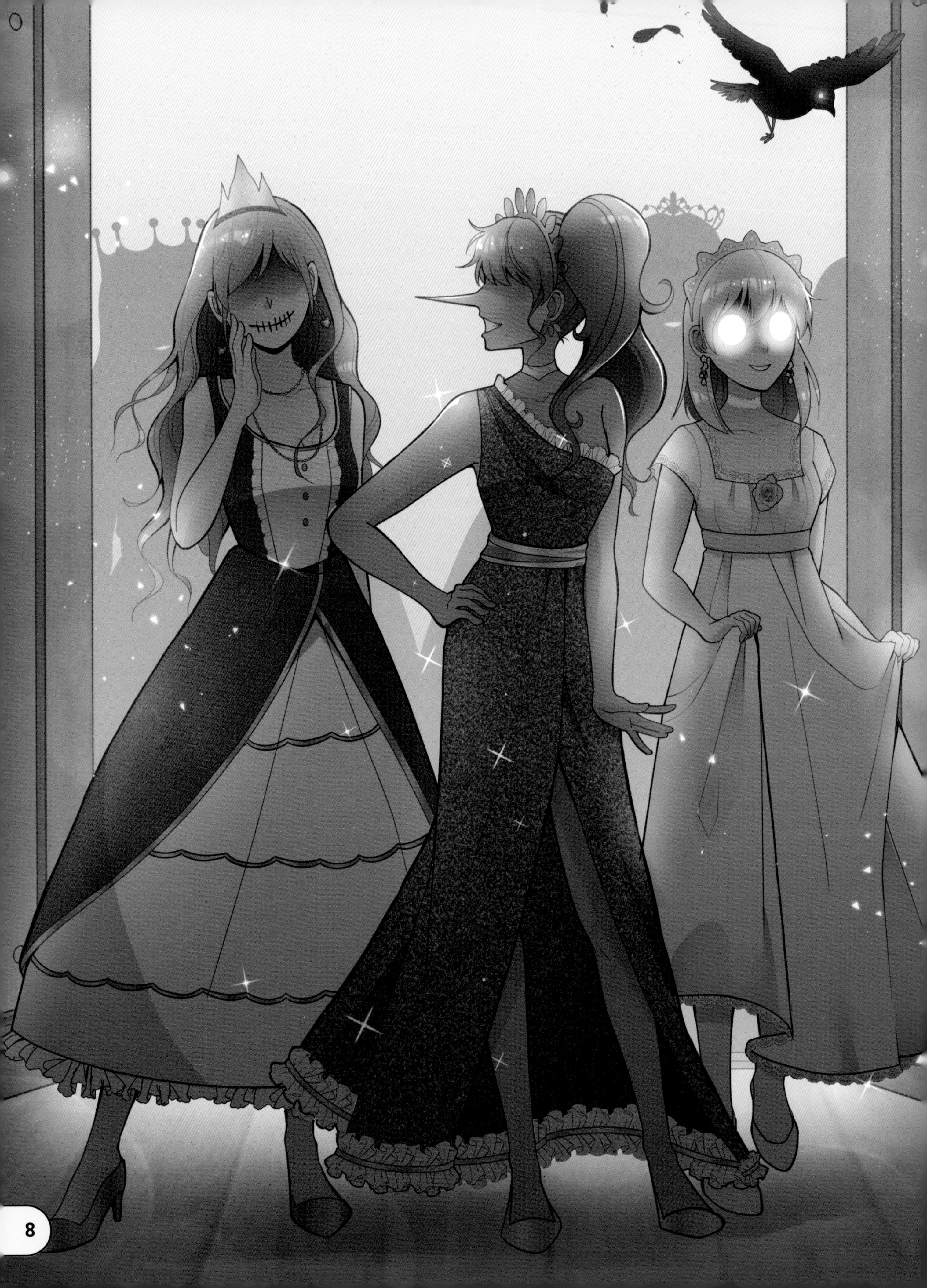

THE CHARACTERS

Meet the cast of Cursed Princess Club.

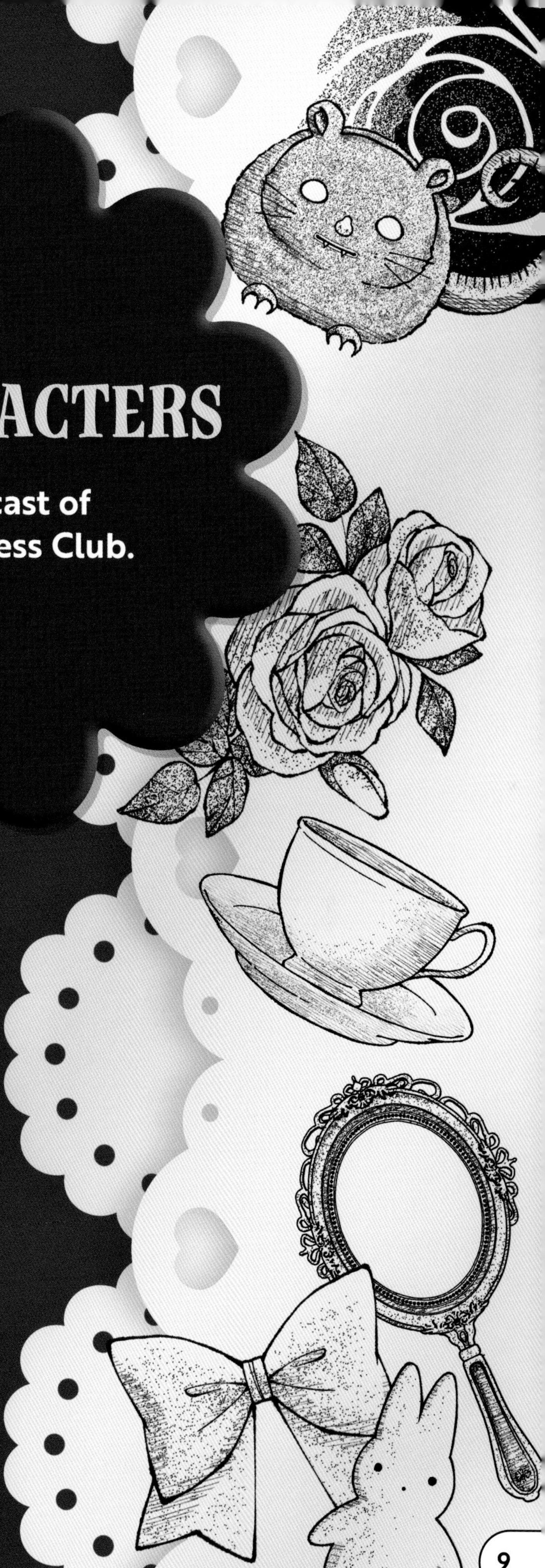

GWENDOLYN "GWEN"

Abilities

Gwen doesn't exhibit any typical princess abilities like her sisters but instead is extremely practical and creative. She excels in arts and crafts. And she has a kindness in her heart that is unparalleled.

Background

Gwen spent her early years sheltered by her father and siblings in the Pastel Kingdom, completely unaware that her strange appearance was abnormal. It wasn't until she was betrothed to a prince from the Plaid Kingdom that she began to understand she was different. This revelation prompted Gwen to start grappling with some major existential questions—but it also prompted an invitation to the Cursed Princess Club, a group of princesses who found themselves situated outside the royal norm in one way or another.

Appearance

Unlike the rest of her family, Gwen's appearance is strange and monstrous. She has sickly greenish skin and hair, sharp teeth, and slightly pointed ears. She sews a lot of her own clothing and likes to dress in an innocent and girly style that Aurelia (a temperamental member of the Cursed Princess Club) sometimes accuses of being "toddler"-like.

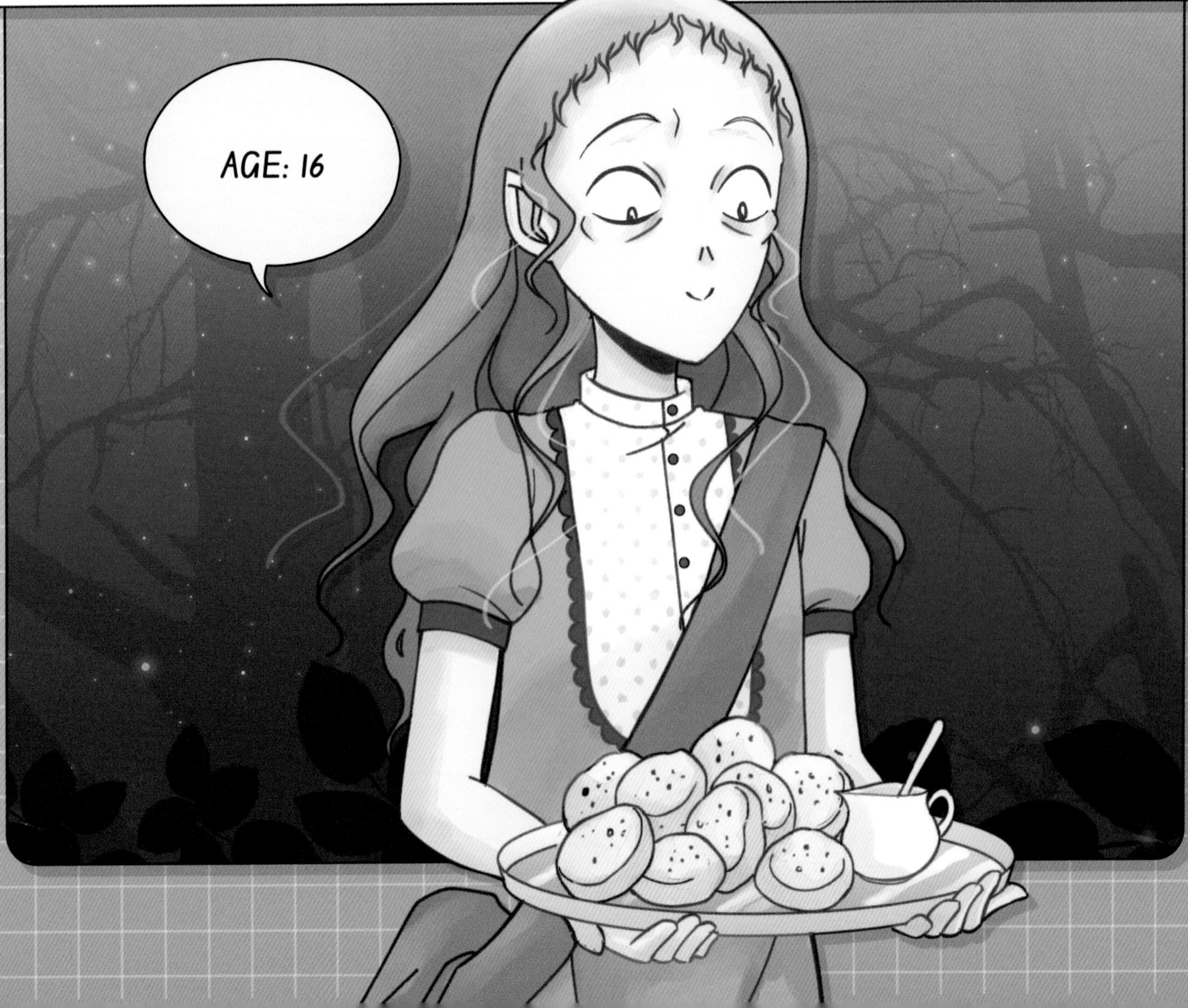
AGE: 16

COLOR PALETTE

HAIR HIGHLIGHT	HAIR MIDTONE	EYES	SKIN
#EBF4CA	#9AAB87	#393A34	#F5F2DC

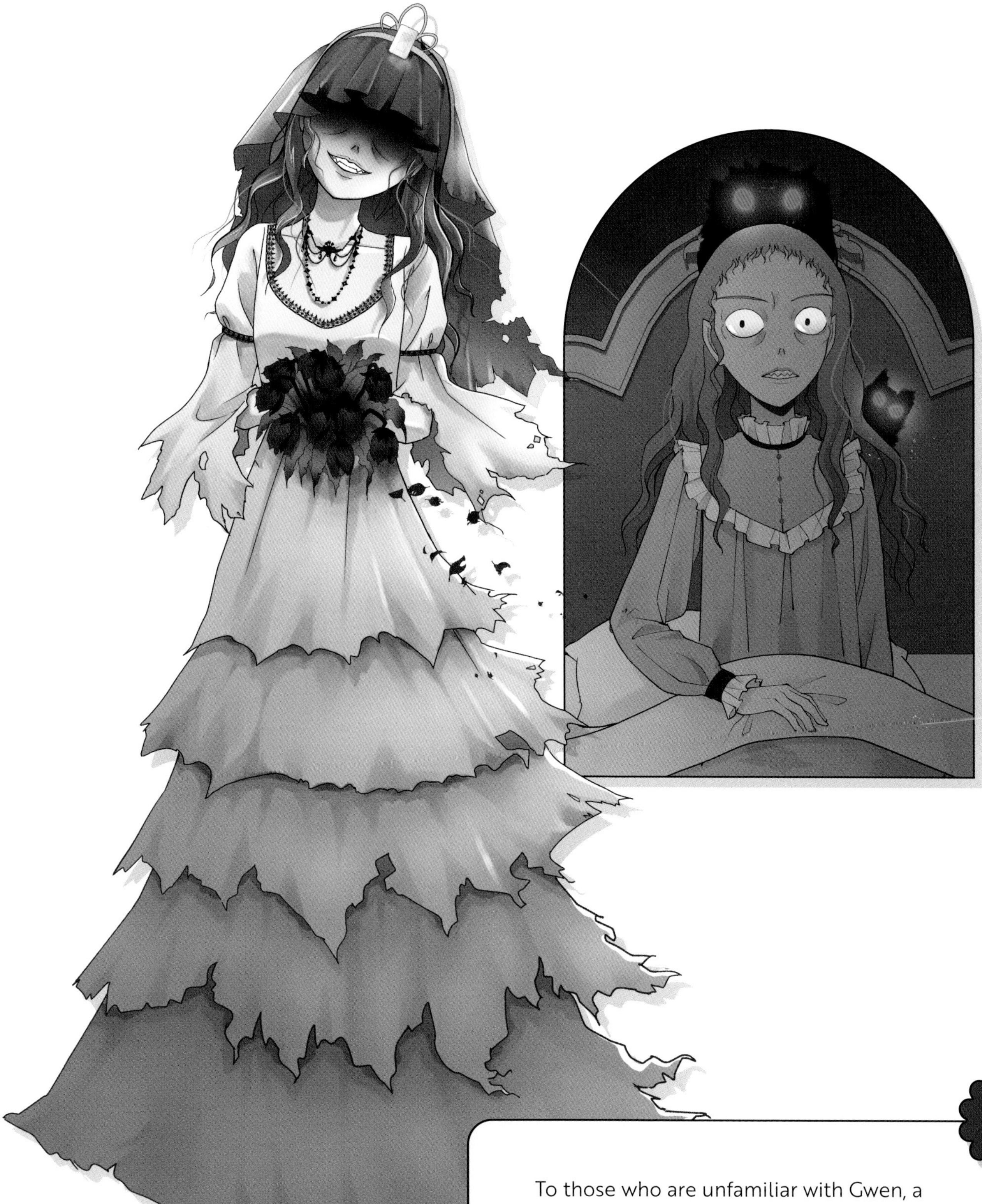

To those who are unfamiliar with Gwen, a first glance of her appearance can tend to be scary or witchlike.

MARIA

Abilities

Maria is so classically beautiful that she frequently finds herself surrounded by helpful woodland creatures that do things like braid her hair and fasten them into her signature buns.

Background

The oldest of the royal siblings in the Pastel Kingdom, Maria is fiercely protective of her family. Maria presents herself as a very polite and put-together princess, but deep down she has a very excitable fangirl side—especially toward her crush, Blaine, to whom she is engaged.

Appearance

Maria is a renowned beauty within the Pastel Kingdom, known for her flowing blonde hair and sparkling blue eyes. She's typically associated with the color blue and prefers dresses and accessories that include that color.

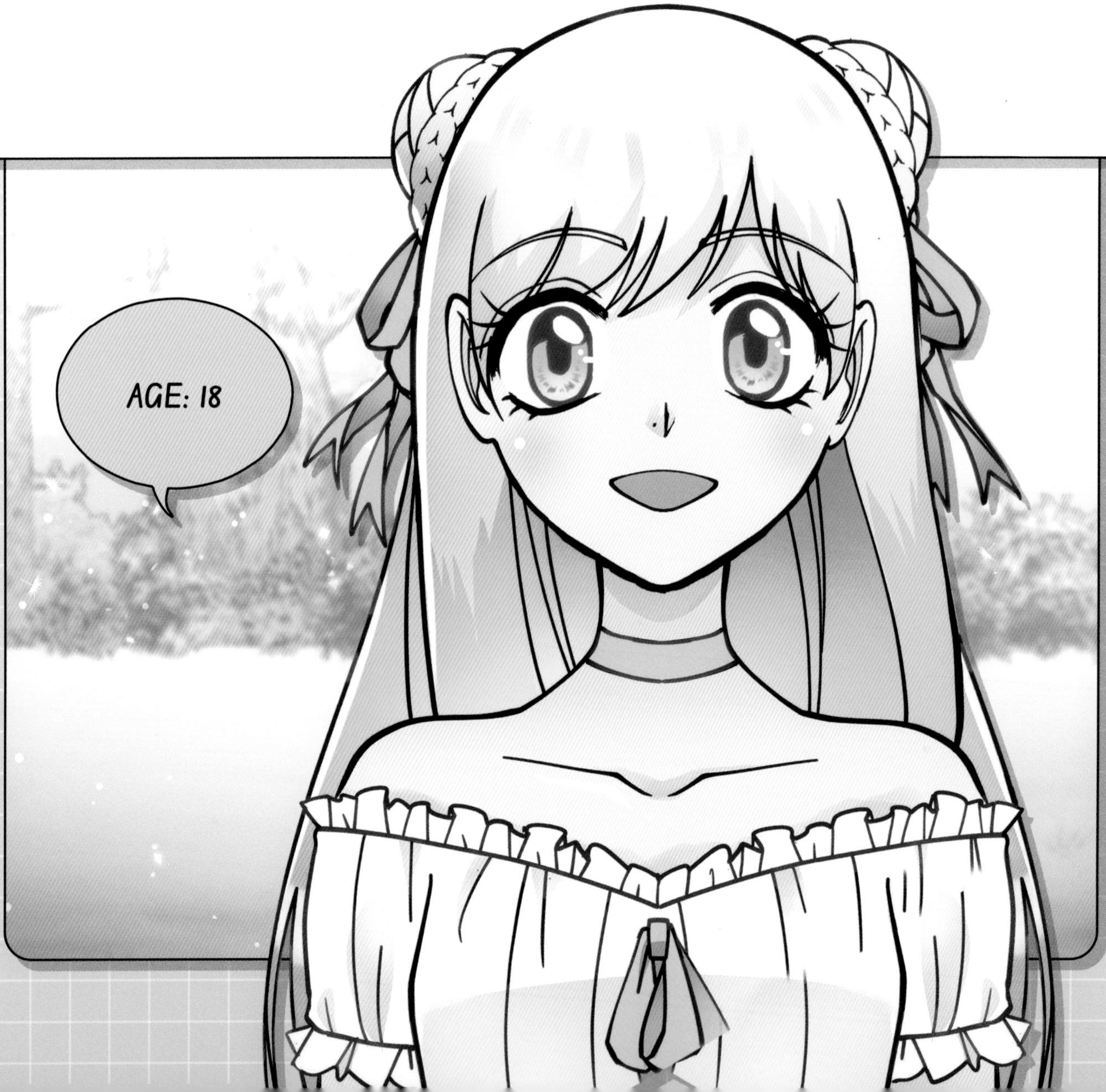
AGE: 18

COLOR PALETTE

HAIR HIGHLIGHT	HAIR MIDTONE	EYES	ACCENT	SKIN
#FDFDC9	#FAD680	#85F9D4	#83E3FA	#FFF2EF

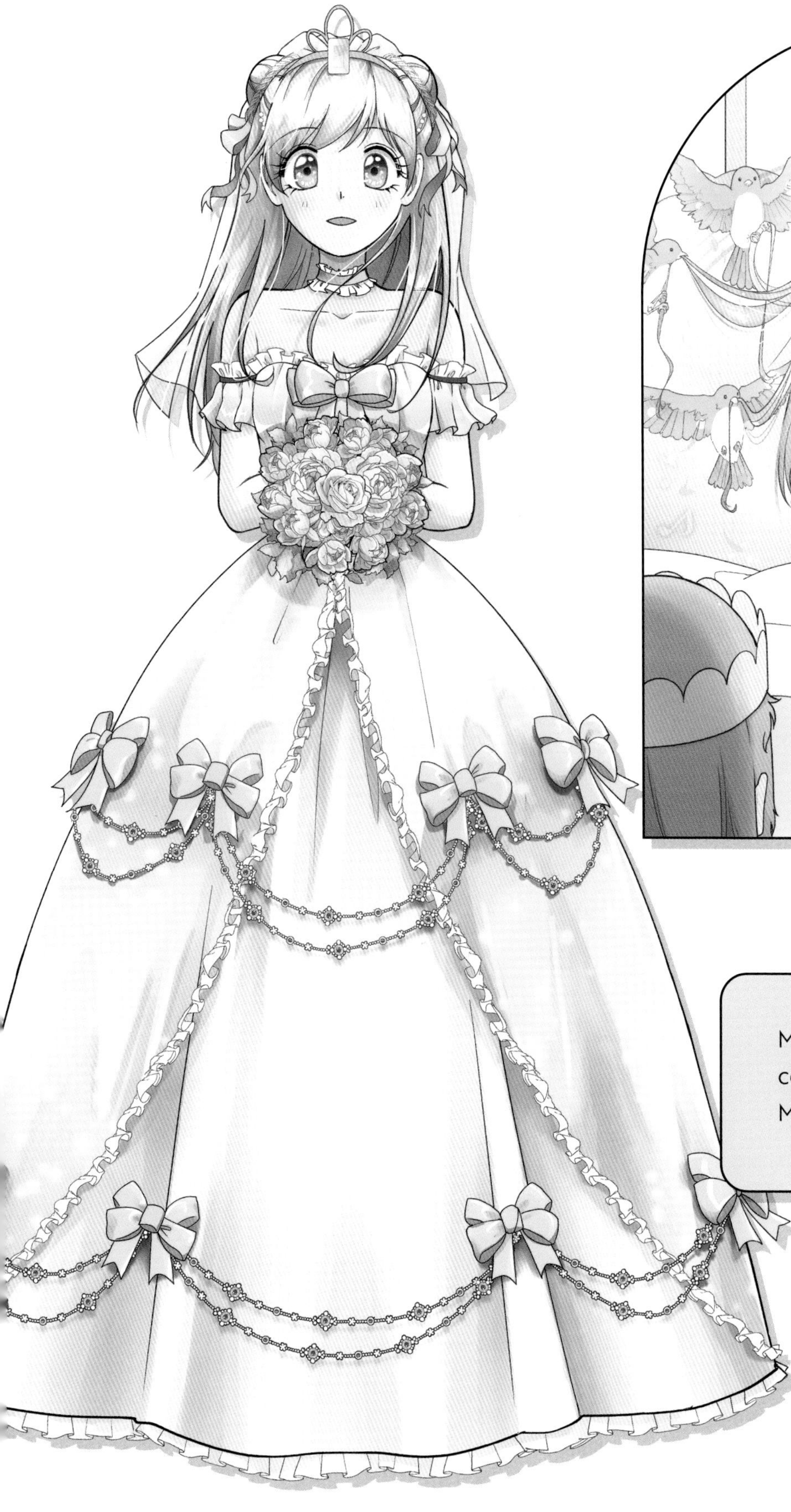

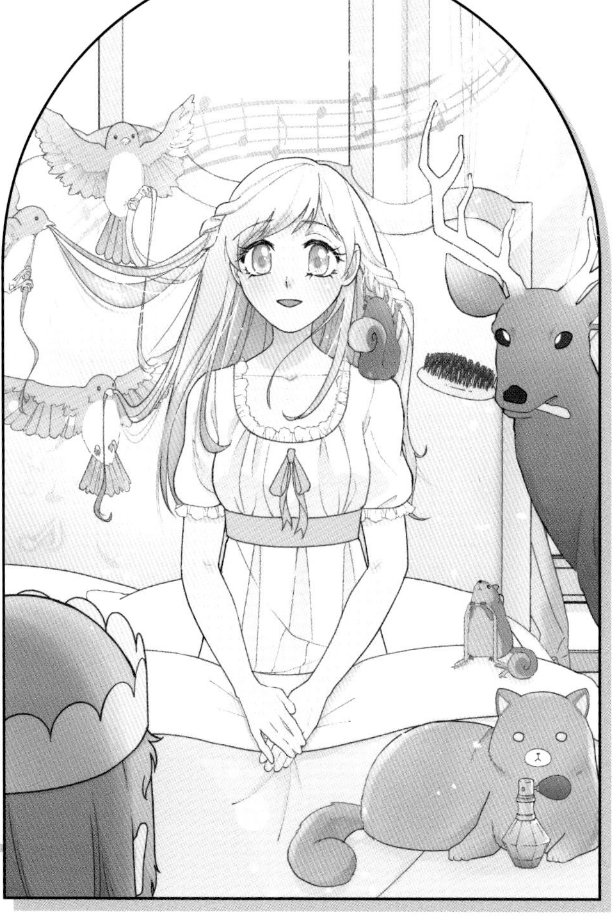

Maria's appearance is a combination of Sailor Moon and Cinderella.

LORENA

Abilities

Like her sister Maria, Lorena is so classically beautiful that the laws of nature seem to bend to her will. Flowers bloom spontaneously around her.

Background

Lorena is the middle daughter in the Pastel Kingdom, and like the rest of her family, is both deeply compassionate and fiercely loyal. Unlike Maria, however, Lorena tends to be a bit more open and less sophisticated in public, making her come across as a bit more brash and energetic when compared to her siblings.

Appearance

Lorena has wavy, lavender hair and sparkling blue eyes. Her wardrobe mostly consists of pink and purple dresses, and she frequently accessories with flower crowns, thanks to the fact she's never hurting for flowers to pick in her general vicinity.

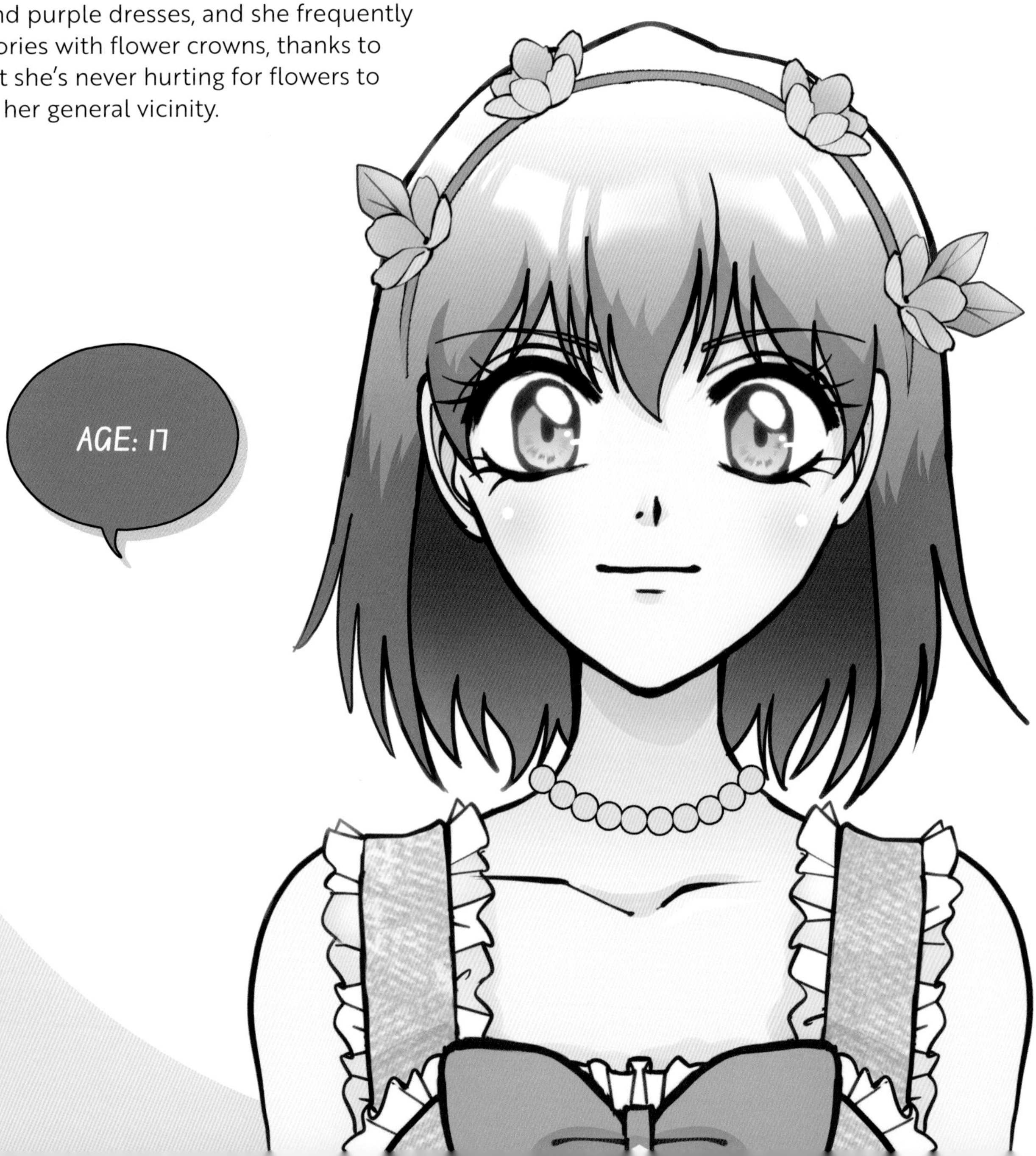
AGE: 17

COLOR PALETTE

HAIR HIGHLIGHT	HAIR MIDTONE	EYES	ACCENT	SKIN
#DCC6E3	#9D79AA	#48D4EE	#F5DEF7	#FFF2EF

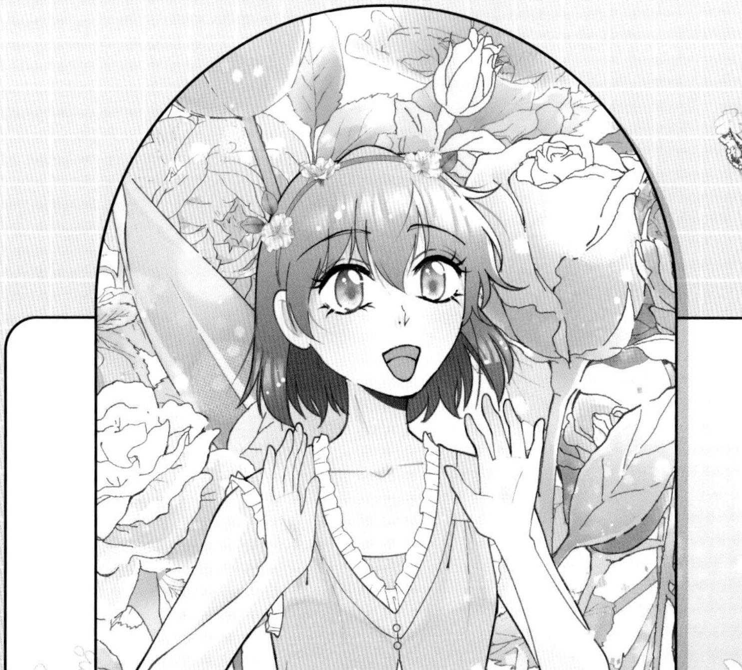

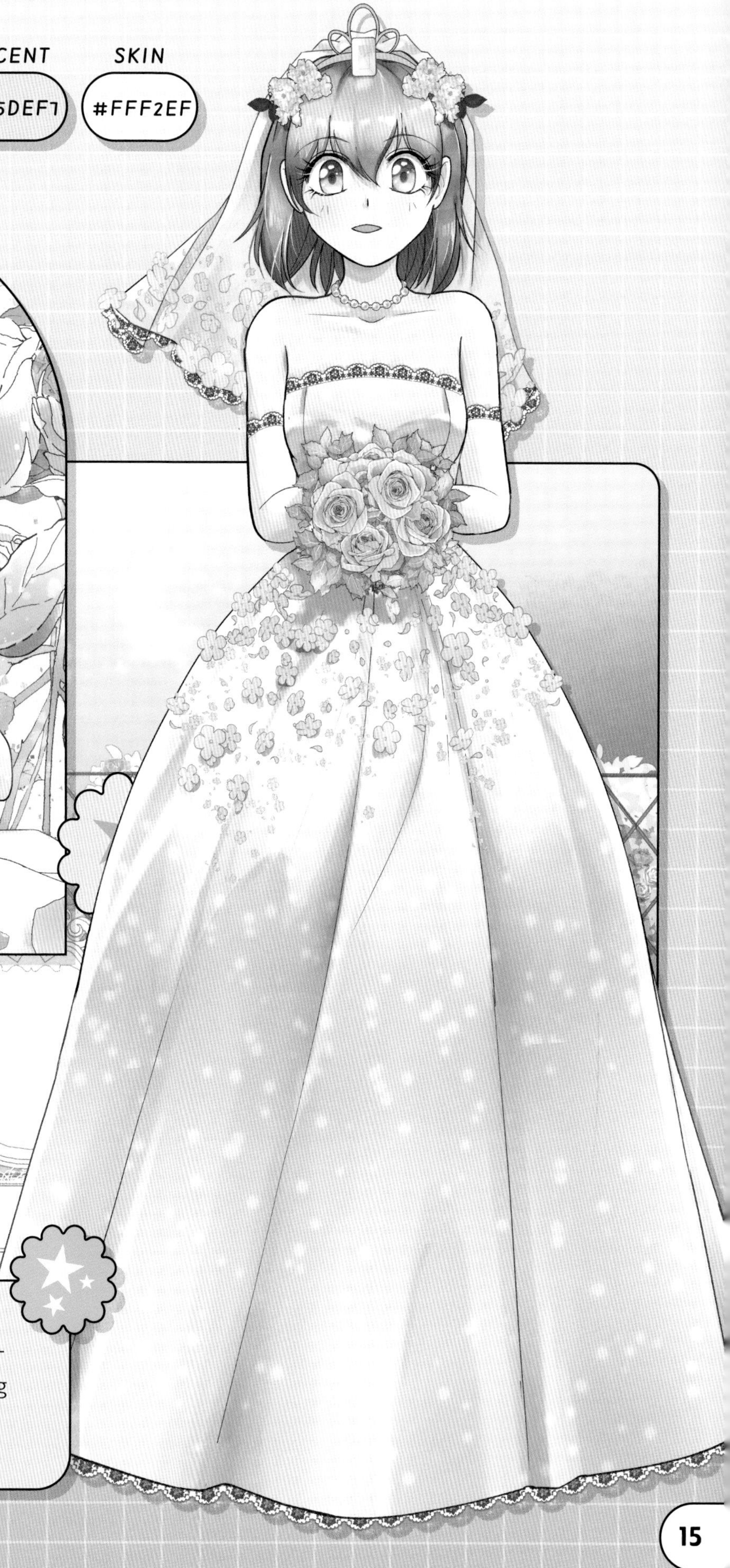

Lorena is an athletic, combat strategy-loving tomboy but also enjoys wearing lots of florals, pearls, and dresses.

JAMIE

Abilities

Similar to his older sisters, Jamie is so beautiful that he gives off literal sparkles and has a slight glowing light, even in the dark. He also has the ability to sense and "taste" the emotions that went into any food he eats, which comes in handy because being a food critic is one of his hobbies.

Background

Jamie has a more laid-back and nonchalant personality compared to his sisters, thanks to the fact that their father's strict and protective parenting didn't extend to him as much as it did to the princesses. He was more able to interact with the outside world and gain a more varied perspective. Because of this, and despite his young age, Jamie often acts as a very willing distraction and scapegoat for his sisters, performing all sorts of outlandish feats in order to distract prying eyes away from them when they might need it.

Appearance

Jamie has short pink hair and bright lavender eyes. He is almost always shown glowing or sparkling and usually dresses in either a princely white collared shirt or in stylish casual clothes in shades of pink. He's the tallest of all his siblings despite being the second youngest.

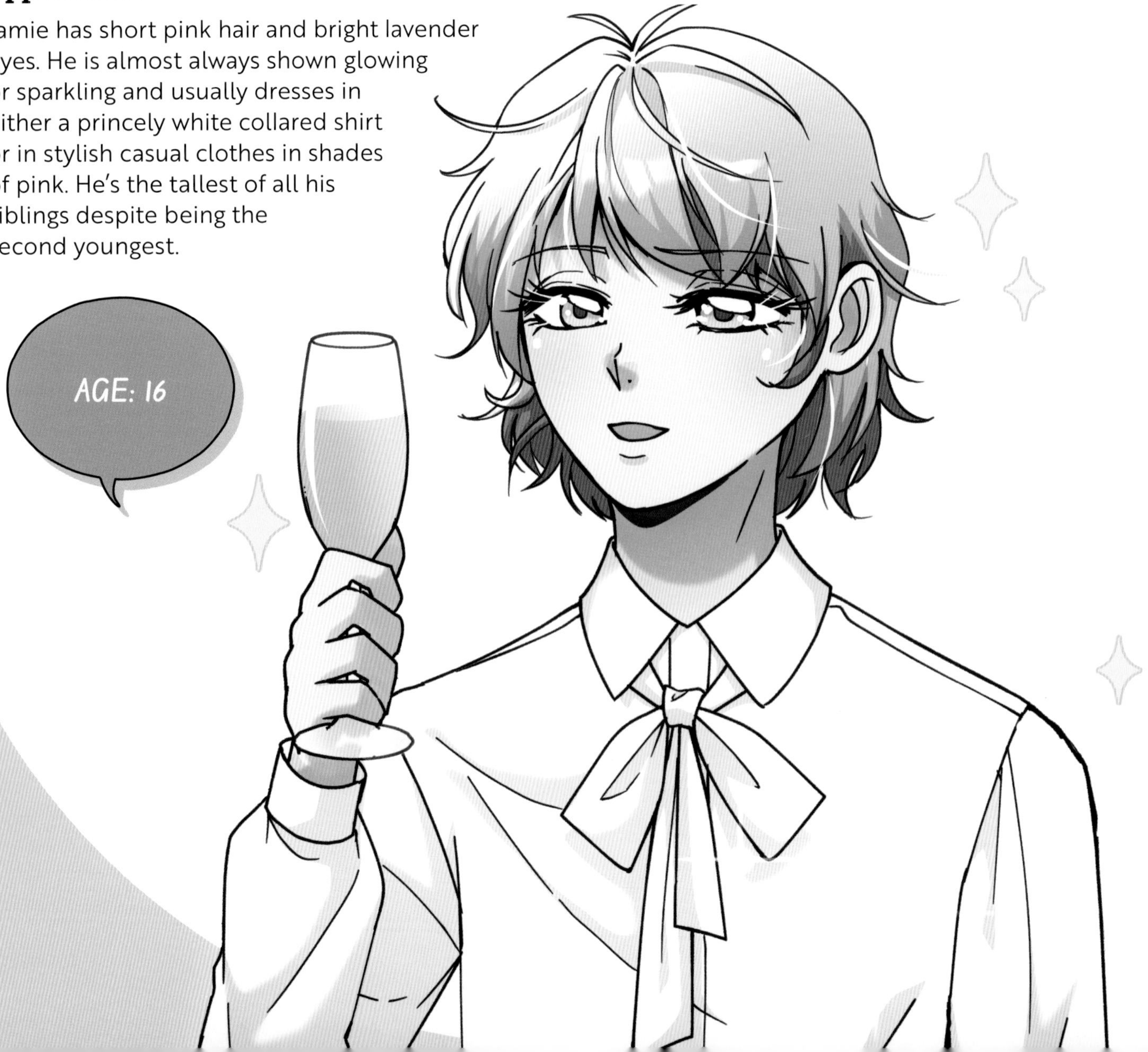
AGE: 16

COLOR PALETTE

HAIR HIGHLIGHT	HAIR MIDTONE	EYES	SKIN
#FFE3F4	#FF93D9	#D69FF9	#FFF2EF

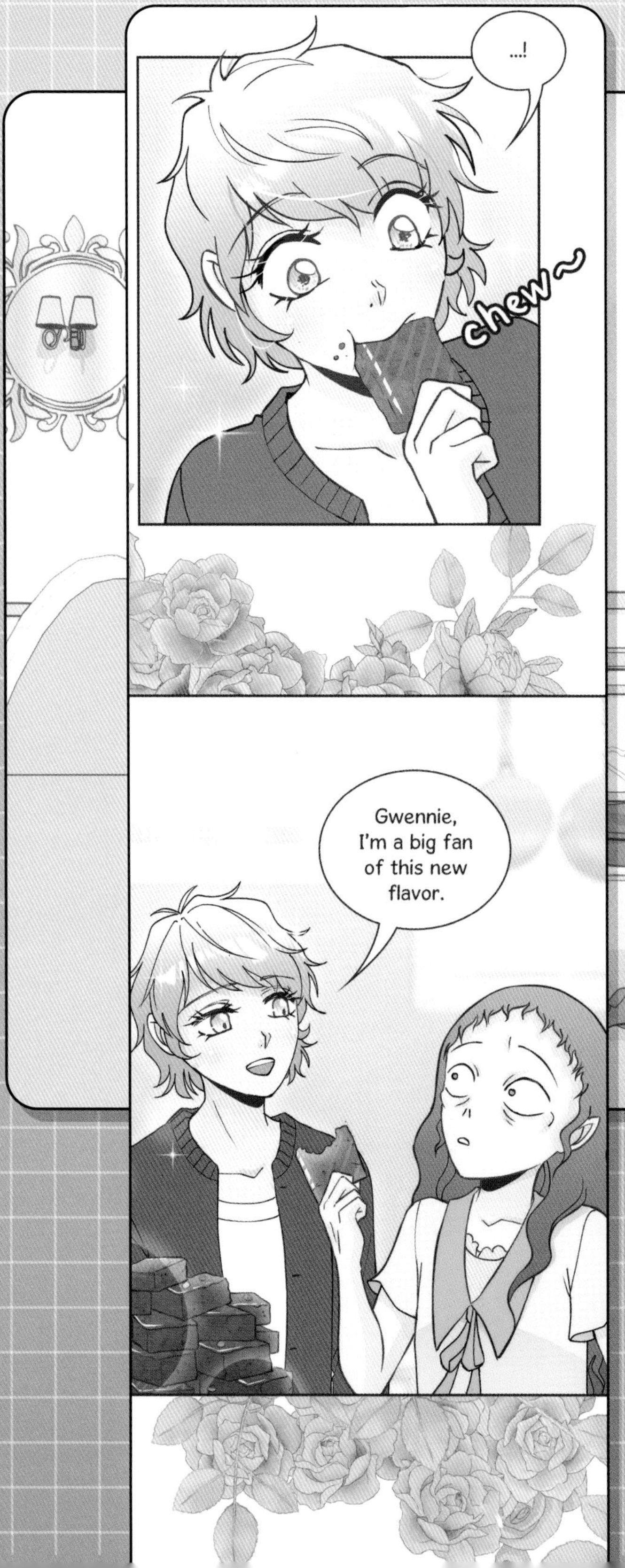

...!
chew~
Gwennie, I'm a big fan of this new flavor.

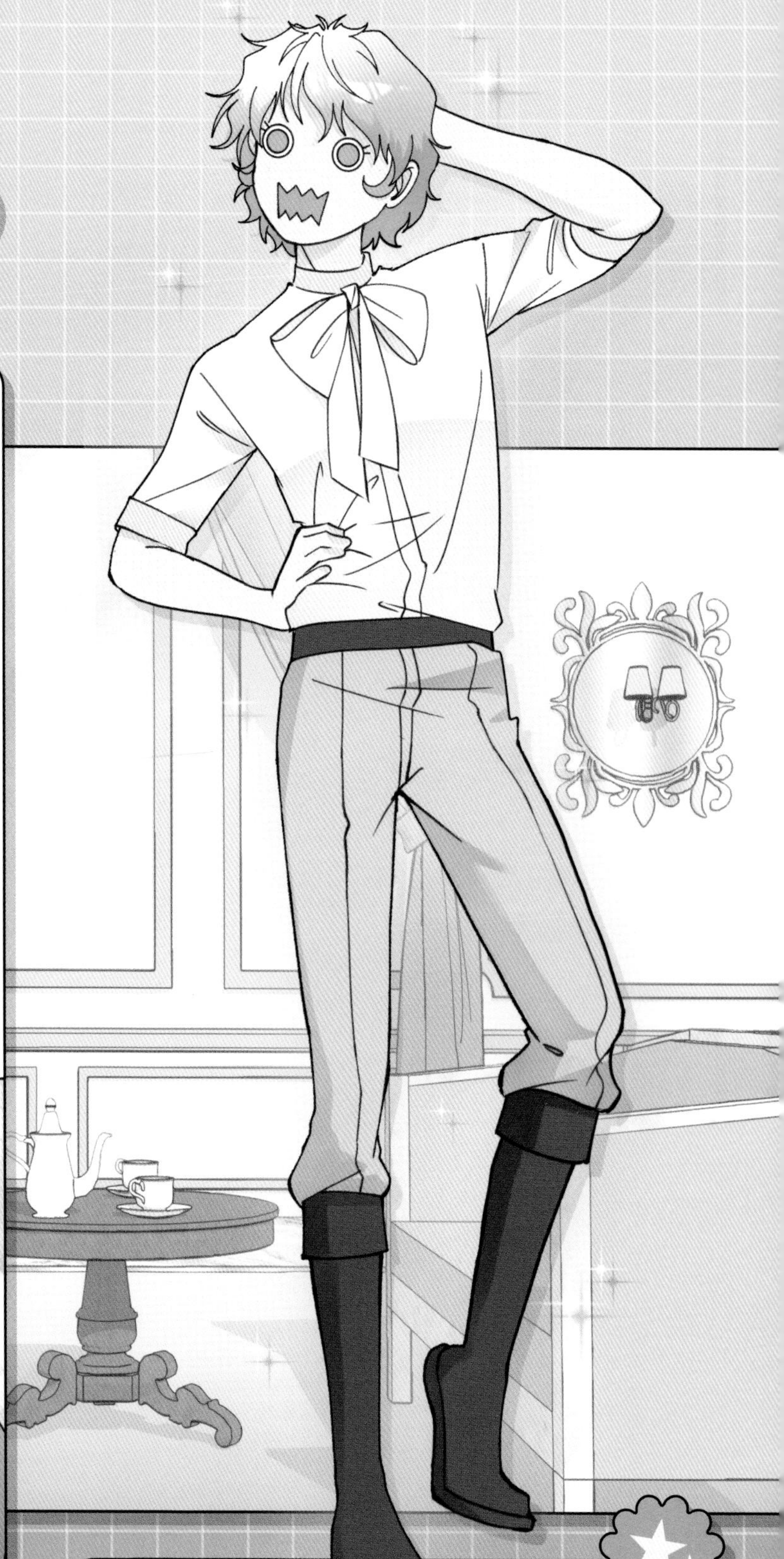

If anyone tries to mess with him—or worse, with his sisters—Jamie becomes devilishly mischievous, which the Pastel Kingdom's royal painter, Leopold, terrifyingly refers to as "pink demon" mode.

FREDERICK

Background

The youngest prince from the Plaid Kingdom, Frederick is an anxious and reserved boy who struggles to assert himself, especially compared to his older brothers. He was bullied as a child, which prompted his love of more introverted activities such as reading, rather than more "princely" pursuits such as fighting or academics. Frederick sees himself as a failure compared to his brothers, whom he believed have accomplished much more notable things. Frederick is engaged to Gwen and was initially very taken aback, even frightened, of her strange appearance.

Appearance

Frederick has messy blond hair that is always sticking up at awkward angles and green eyes. He wears a green uniform with a plain white shirt under the jacket.

AGE: 17

COLOR PALETTE

HAIR HIGHLIGHT	HAIR MIDTONE	EYES	ACCENT	SKIN
#FFFBAD	#E5BA3B	#40C87A	#399E7A	#FFE7DA

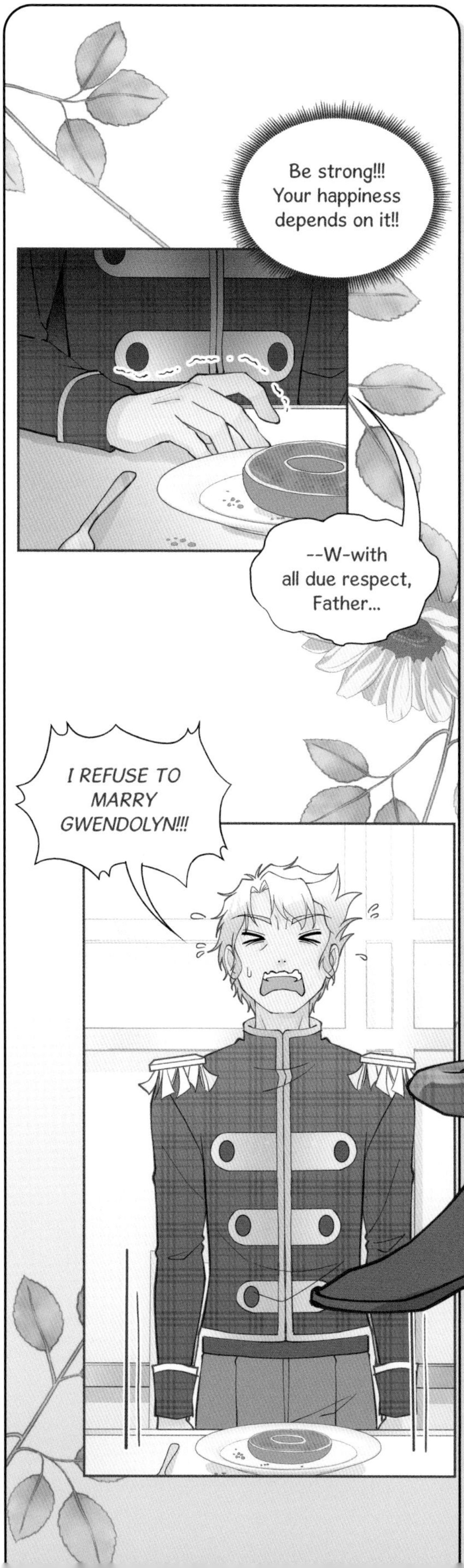
Be strong!!! Your happiness depends on it!!
--W-with all due respect, Father...
I REFUSE TO MARRY GWENDOLYN!!!

For special occasions, Frederick will forgo his royal jacket for formal wear in various shades of green.

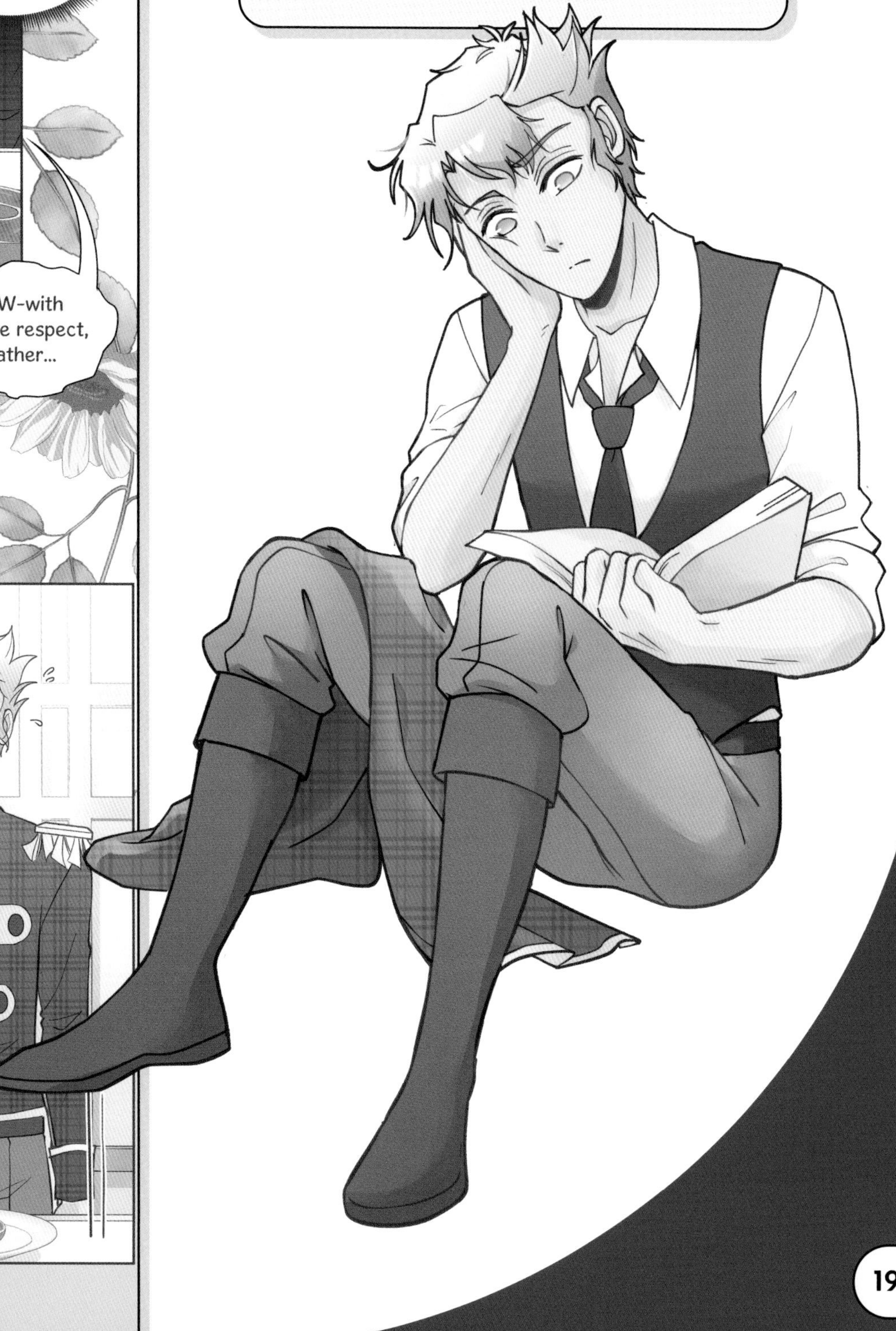

LANCE

Background

Lance is more brawn than brains, especially compared to his brothers within the Plaid Kingdom. This doesn't mean he's necessarily unintelligent, but his interests lay more in things such as sports rather than strategy. He can come off as rude and boastful and often acts before he thinks. Lance is engaged to Lorena, who wound up challenging many of his assumptions about women, thanks to her own innate abilities in sports and fighting.

Appearance

Lance has closely cropped silver hair, gray eyes, and sharp features. He has a scar on his right cheek that curves over his cheekbone, close to his eye. He typically wears a blue jacket over a white V-neck shirt.

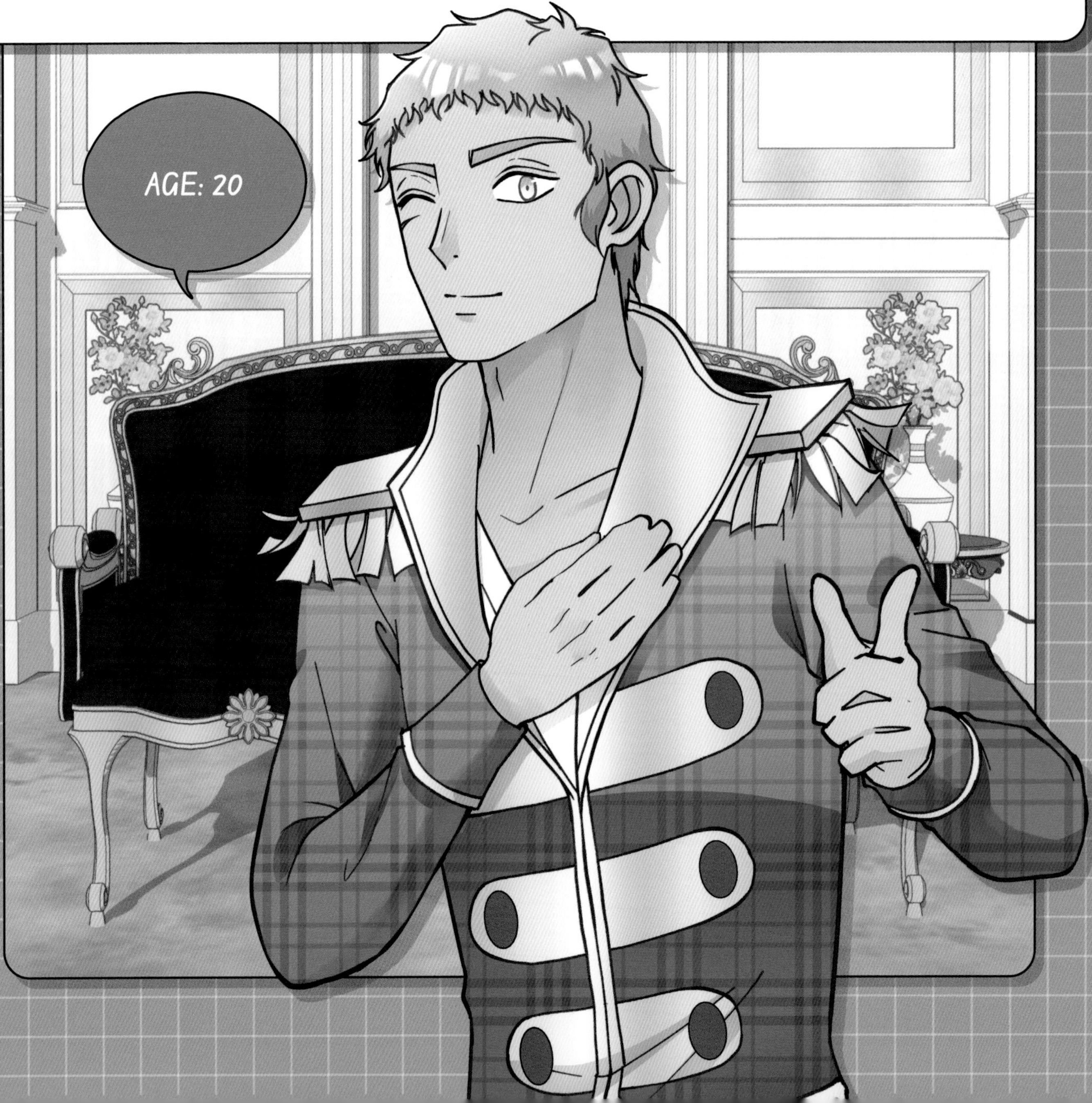
AGE: 20

COLOR PALETTE

HAIR HIGHLIGHT	HAIR MIDTONE	EYES	ACCENT	SKIN
#C2C4C7	#A2A4A7	#EBF4FB	#6E8DCC	#F0D7AC

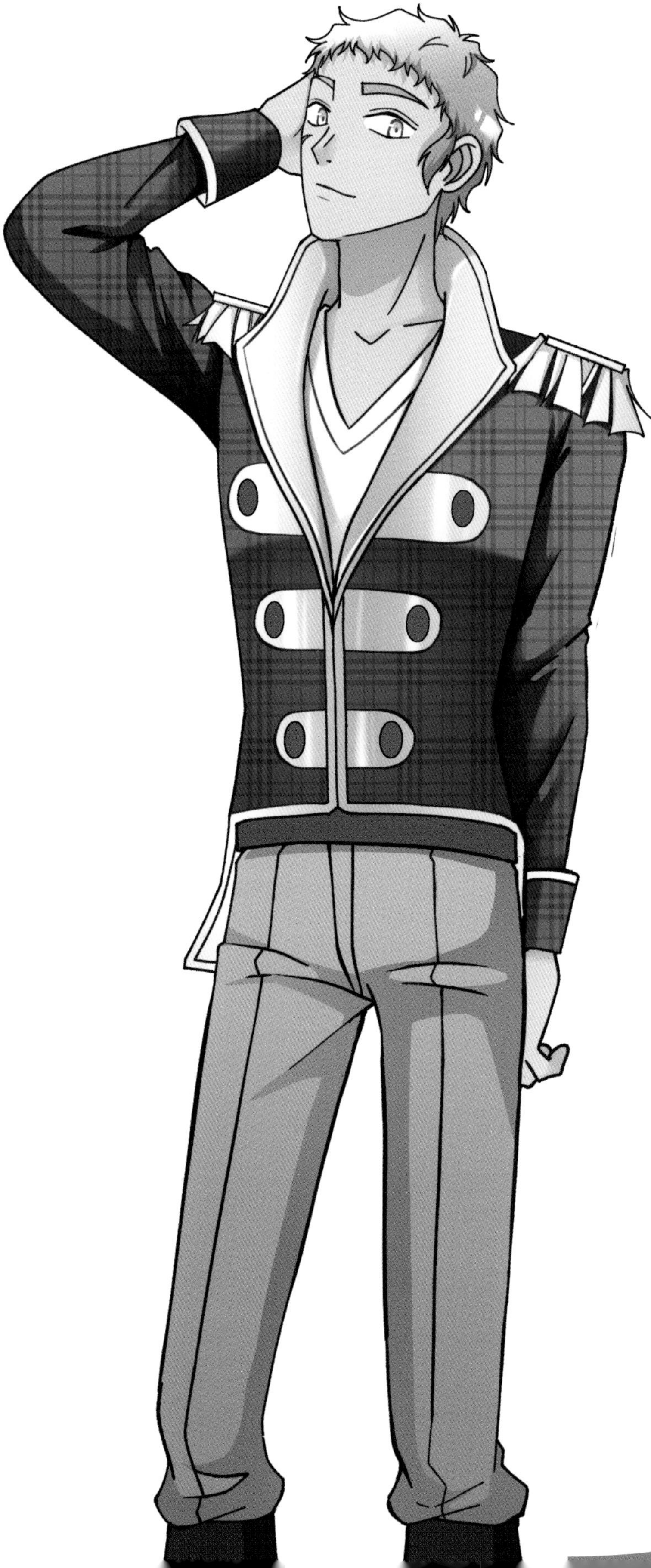

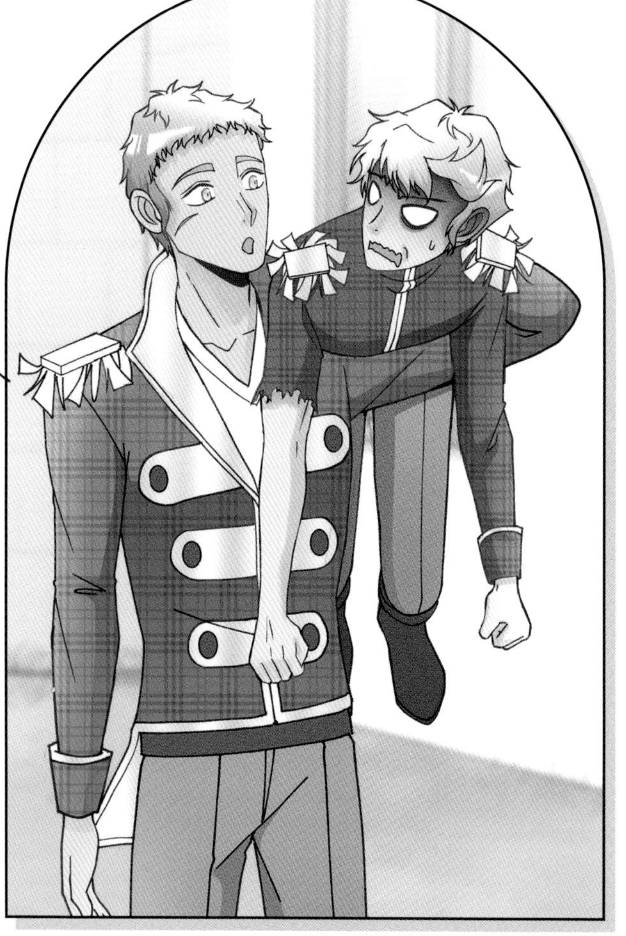

Lance can easily pick up Frederick and often affectionately refers to him as "lil' bro," much to Frederick's agitation.

BLAINE

Background

Blaine is the eldest prince of the Plaid Kingdom and is also widely renowned as an idol, acclaimed pianist, and model Prince Charming. Publicly, he bears this responsibility well, but privately Blaine is deeply insecure about his status and feels a tremendous amount of pressure to live up to people's expectations. Because of this, he often leans into his younger brother's own insecurities to make himself feel a bit better, though over time he's learned to open up emotionally and has been working to overcome some of his more underhanded impulses.

Appearance

Blaine has short brown hair and red eyes. Like his brothers, he is classically handsome, tall, and charming. He wears primarily red and is most often seen in his red plaid uniform, which he keeps clean and well styled.

AGE: 20

COLOR PALETTE

HAIR HIGHLIGHT	HAIR MIDTONE	EYES	ACCENT	SKIN
#DBB1A6	#C58675	#EC6B69	#D95957	#FFE7DA

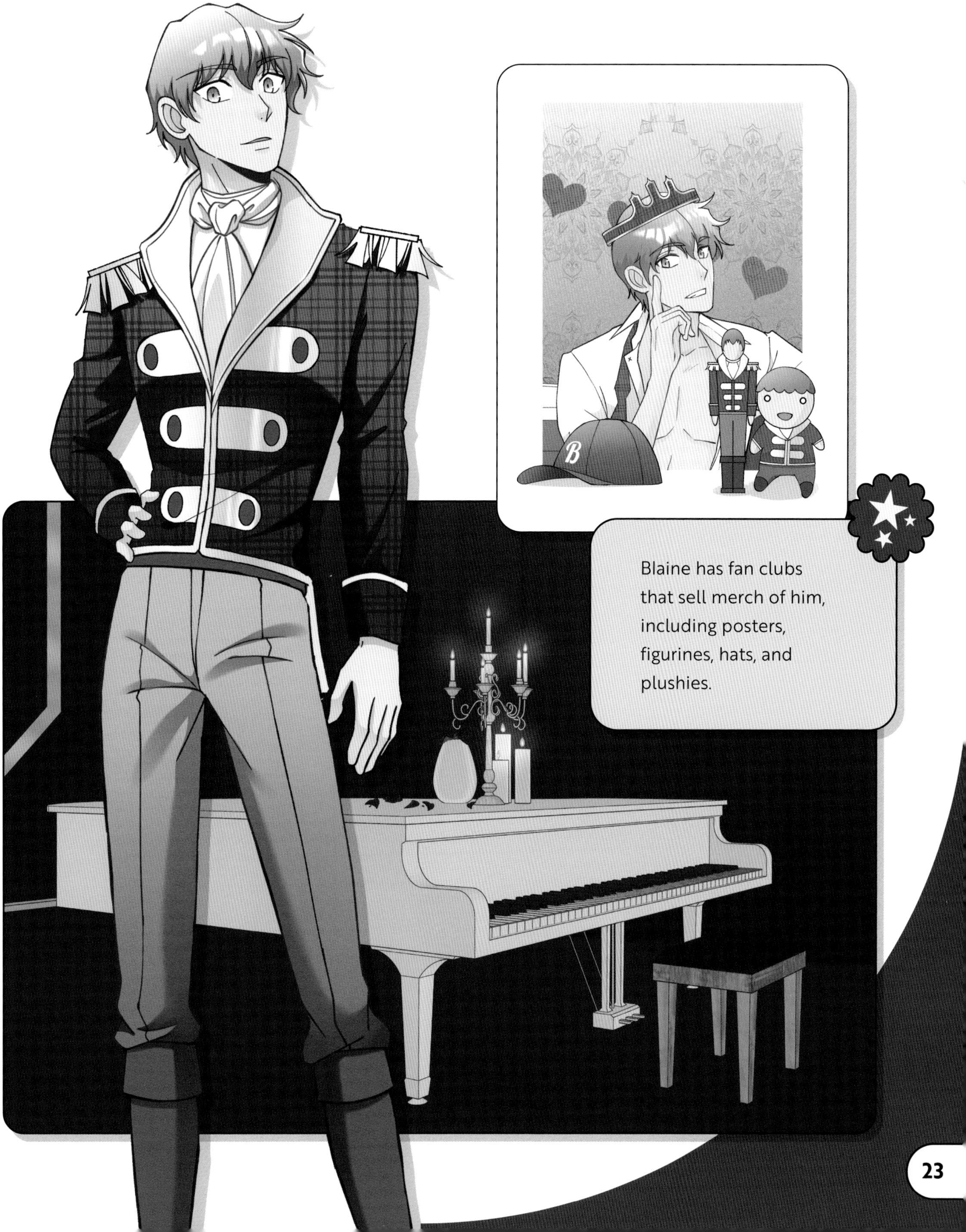

Blaine has fan clubs that sell merch of him, including posters, figurines, hats, and plushies.

PRINCESS CALPERNIA "PREZ"

Abilities

Calpernia bears a were-spider curse, meaning she transforms into a giant, monstrous spider once a month.

Background

Calpernia is the founder of the Cursed Princess Club (CPC). When she was younger, she was the model of a perfect princess. However, when she was betrothed to a prince from a neighboring kingdom whom she did not love, she fell into a depression that her parents tried to cure with the help of a nurse named Asa. Calpernia's nurse soon fell in love with her, much to the ire of her fiancé, who tried to murder Asa with a curse that would turn him into a spider. But instead of hitting Asa, Calpernia jumped in to take the bullet to save Asa's life.

Calpernia's transformation into a were-spider resulted in the death of her fiancé and a scandal that rocked her home, the Polygon Kingdom. She was exiled and moved to establish the CPC as a support group for any princesses who may end up in similar situations for any reason.

Appearance

Calpernia has yellow eyes and steel-blue hair, typically kept up in a bun. She wears a homemade golden crown featuring metal-shaped accents—a nod to her home kingdom, and a spiderweb inspired "widow's veil." She typically dresses in masculine, prince-like clothing and pantsuits in blue, gold, and soot black.

AGE: 25

COLOR PALETTE

HAIR HIGHLIGHT	HAIR MIDTONE	EYES	ACCENT	SKIN
#A8BCE1	#6D96D4	#FFEB95	#F5E4B7	#E7C9C2

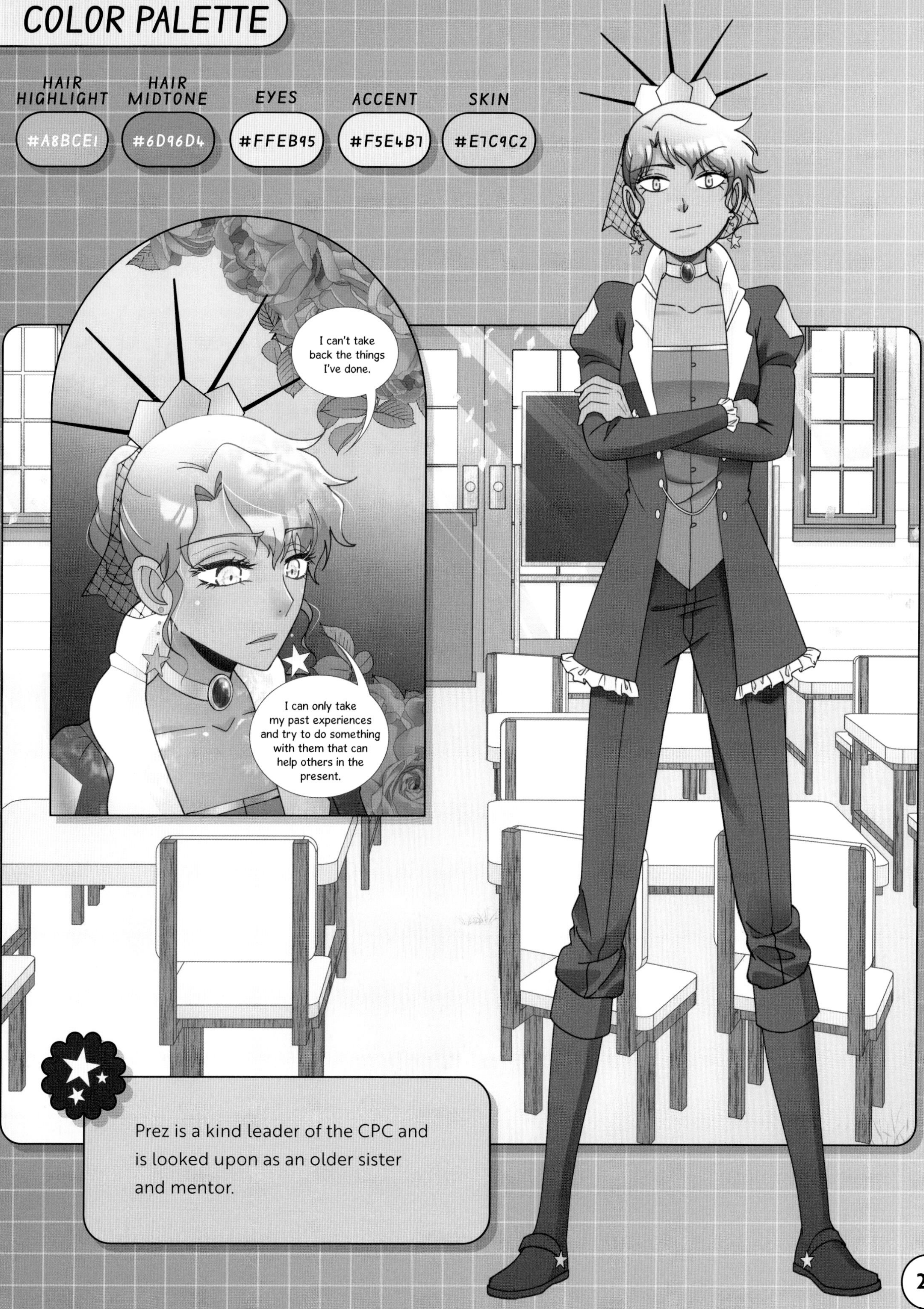

I can't take back the things I've done.
I can only take my past experiences and try to do something with them that can help others in the present.

Prez is a kind leader of the CPC and is looked upon as an older sister and mentor.

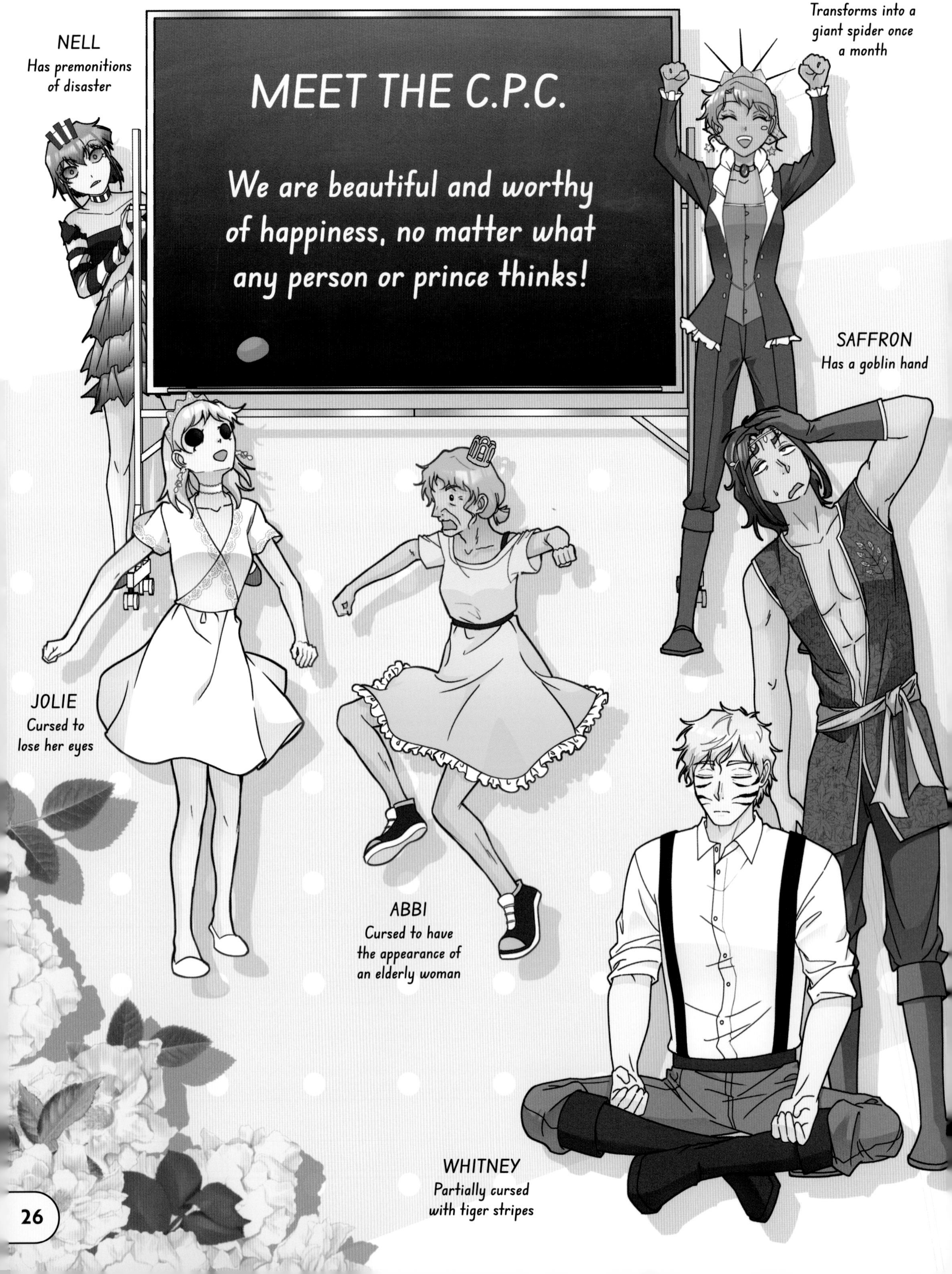

MEET THE C.P.C.
We are beautiful and worthy of happiness, no matter what any person or prince thinks!
NELL
Has premonitions of disaster
PREZ
Transforms into a giant spider once a month
SAFFRON
Has a goblin hand
JOLIE
Cursed to lose her eyes
ABBI
Cursed to have the appearance of an elderly woman
WHITNEY
Partially cursed with tiger stripes

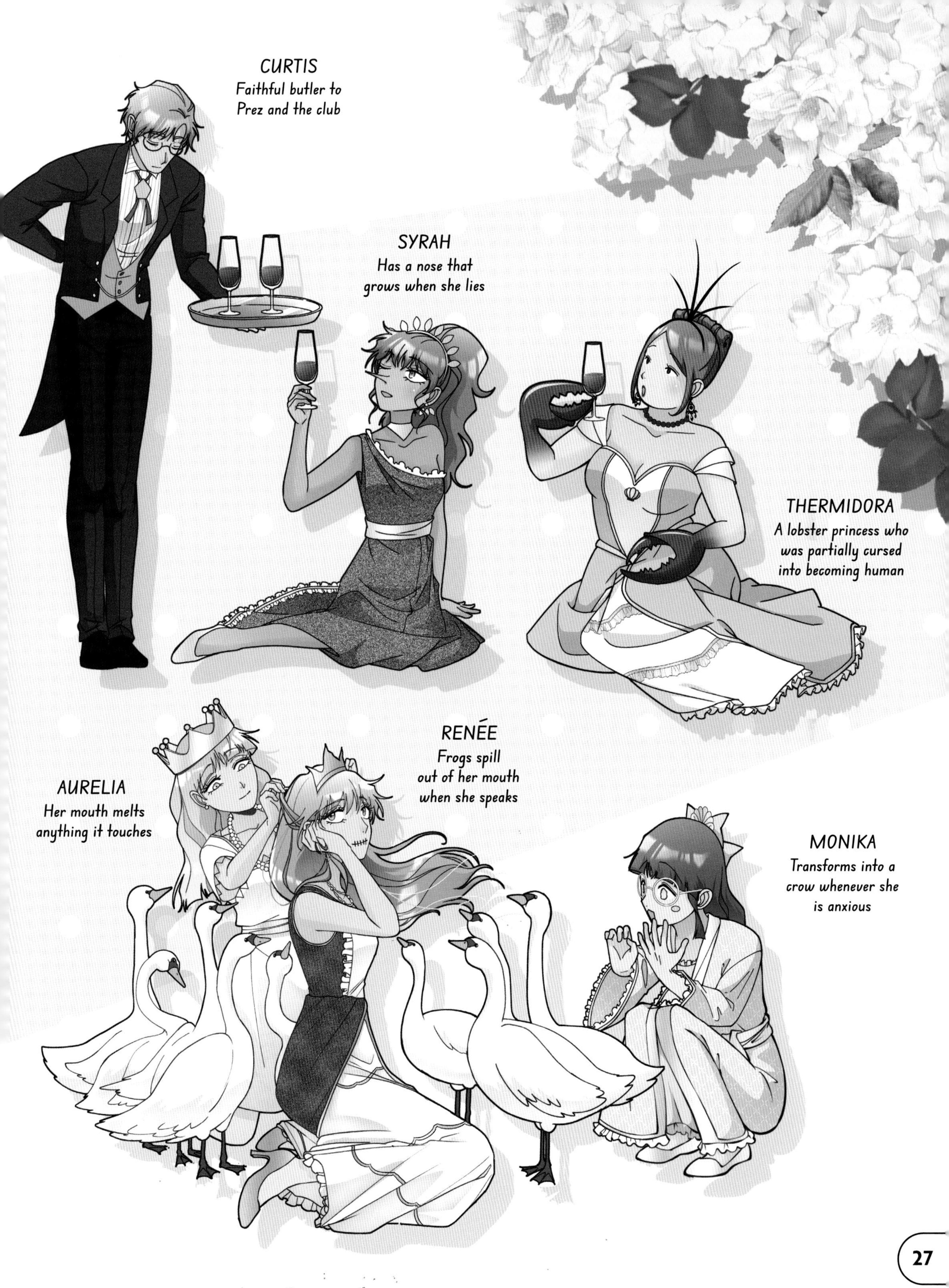
CURTIS
Faithful butler to Prez and the club
SYRAH
Has a nose that grows when she lies
THERMIDORA
A lobster princess who was partially cursed into becoming human
RENÉE
Frogs spill out of her mouth when she speaks
AURELIA
Her mouth melts anything it touches
MONIKA
Transforms into a crow whenever she is anxious

PASTEL KINGDOM CHARACTERS

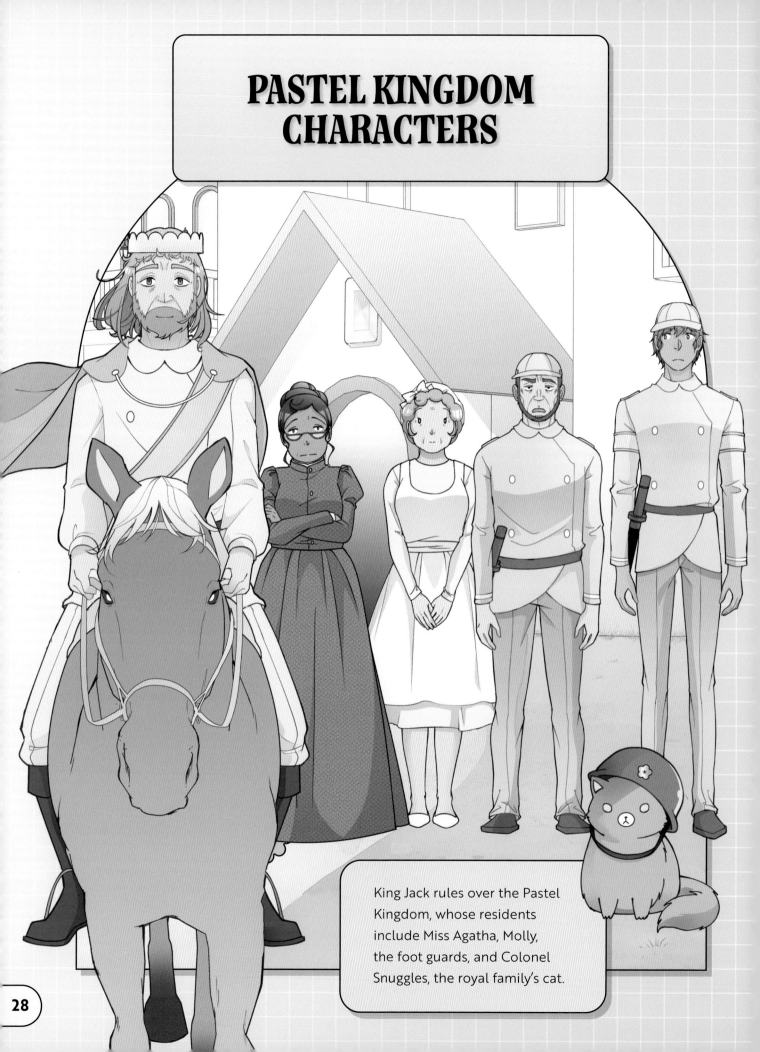

King Jack rules over the Pastel Kingdom, whose residents include Miss Agatha, Molly, the foot guards, and Colonel Snuggles, the royal family's cat.

PLAID KINGDOM CHARACTERS

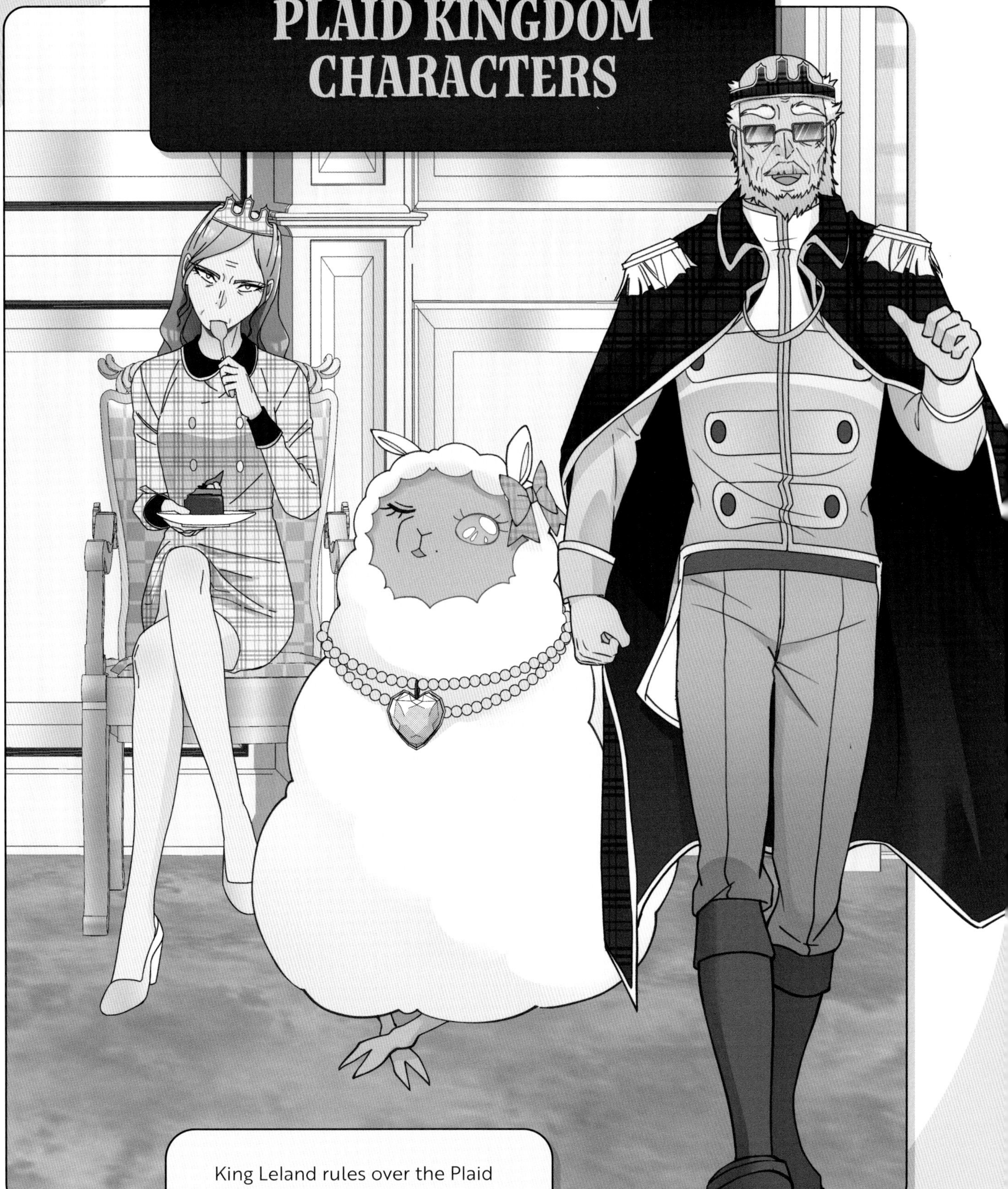

King Leland rules over the Plaid Kingdom with Queen Isolde and Laverne the llama at his side.

CHARACTER HEIGHT CHART

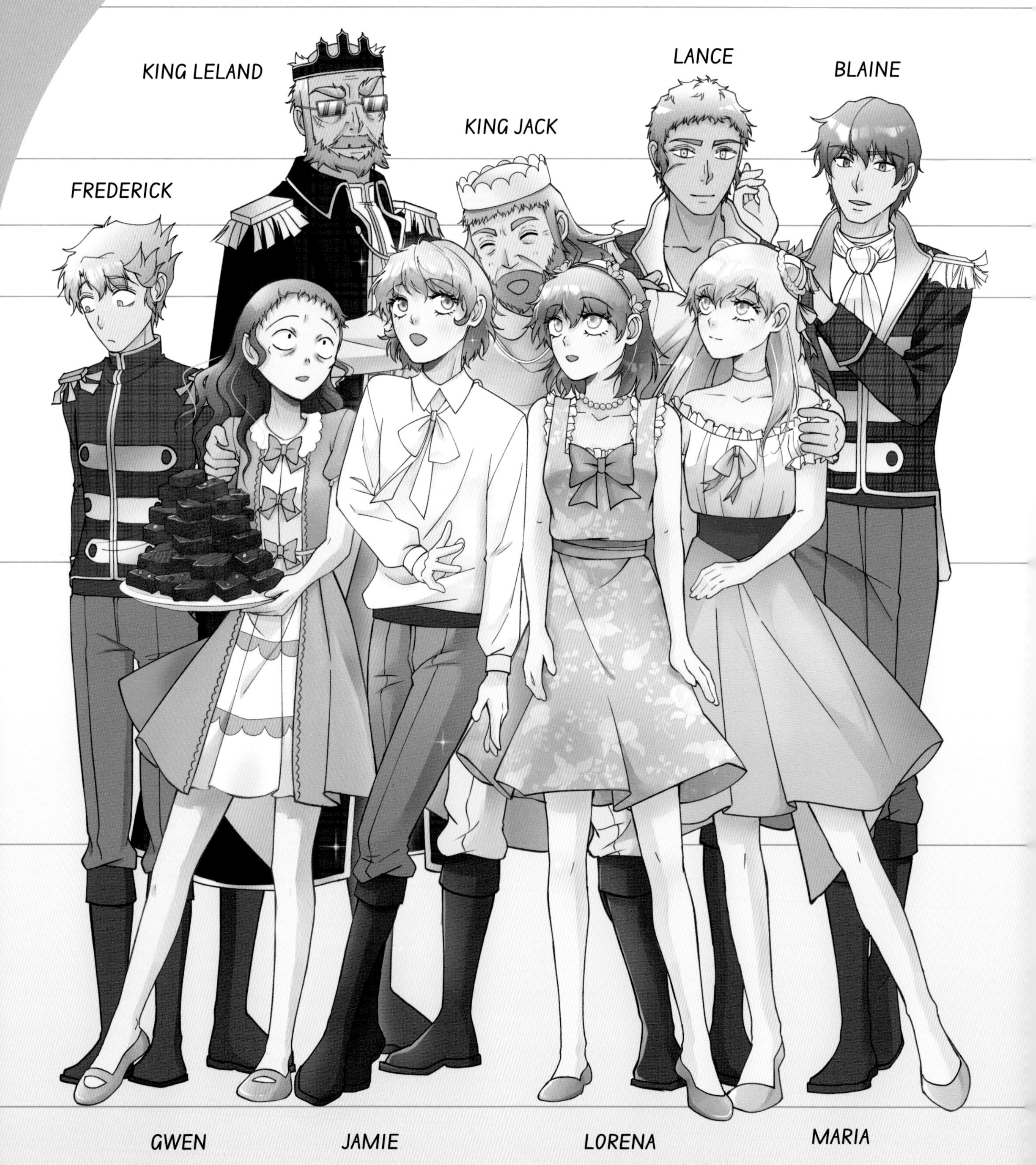
KING LELAND
LANCE
BLAINE
KING JACK
FREDERICK
GWEN
JAMIE
LORENA
MARIA

When developing a cast of characters for a story, it is good to map out how tall they are in relation to each other so you can maintain consistency when drawing them together in various scenes.

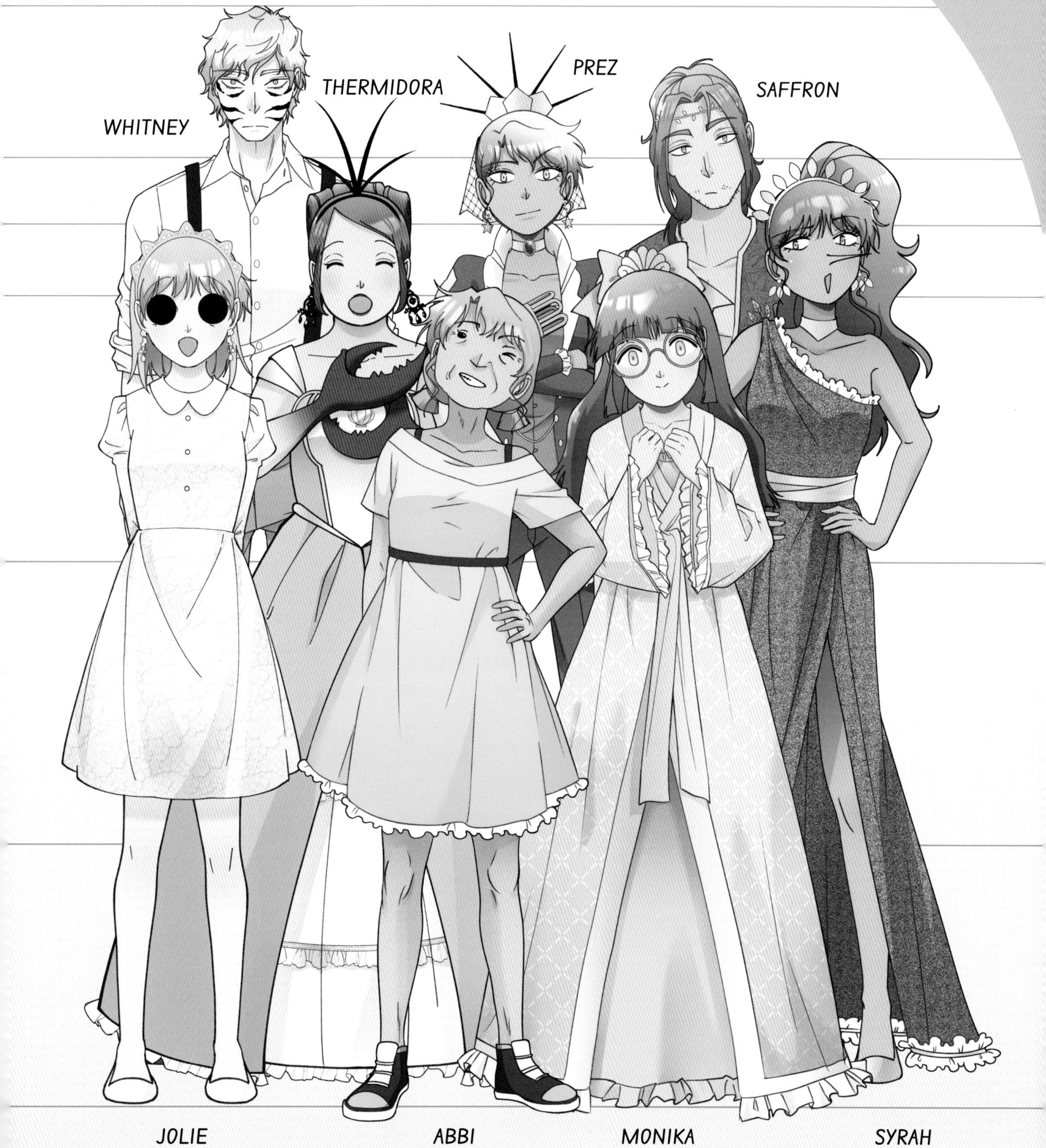
WHITNEY
THERMIDORA
PREZ
SAFFRON
JOLIE
ABBI
MONIKA
SYRAH

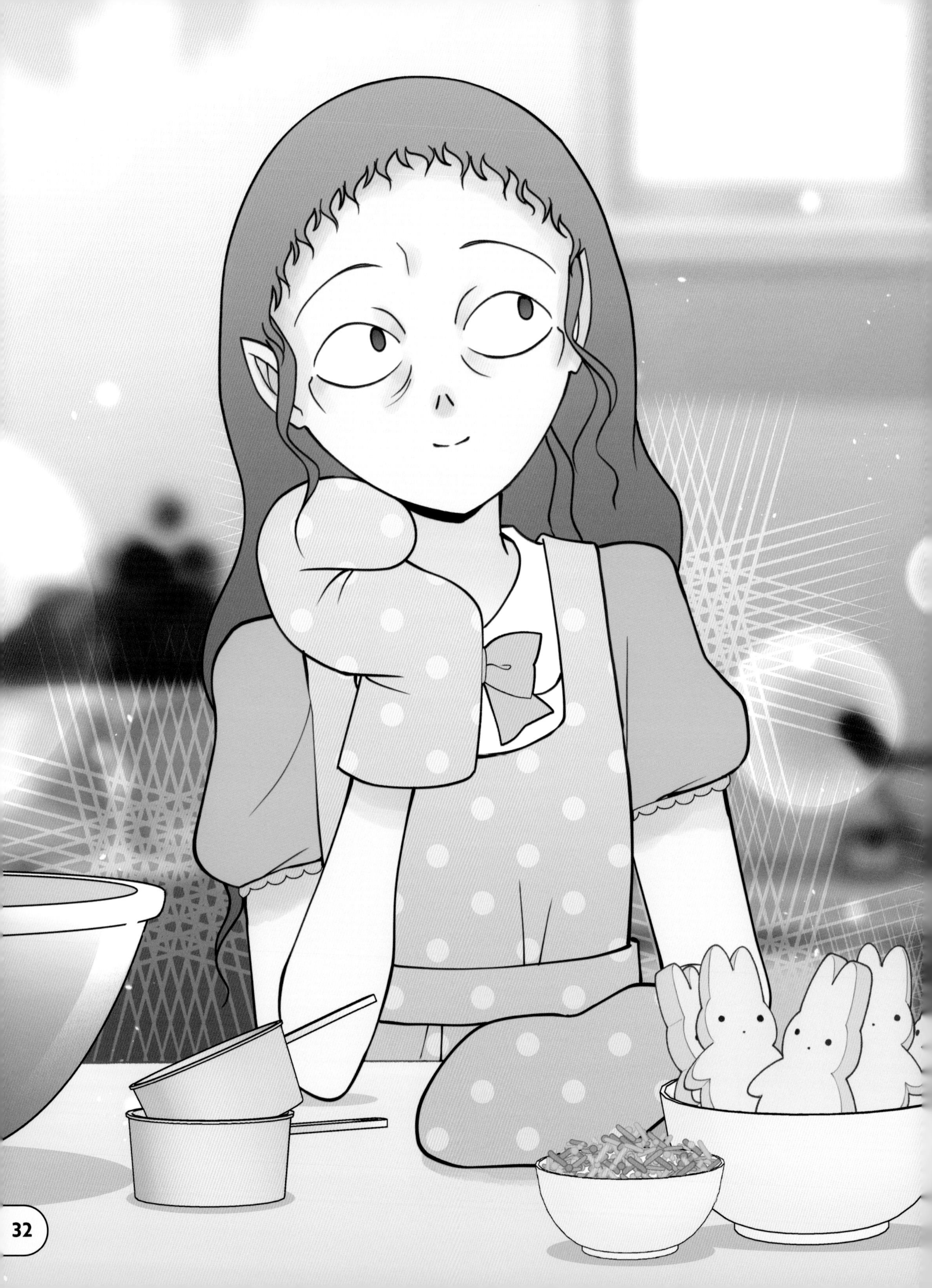

GETTING STARTED

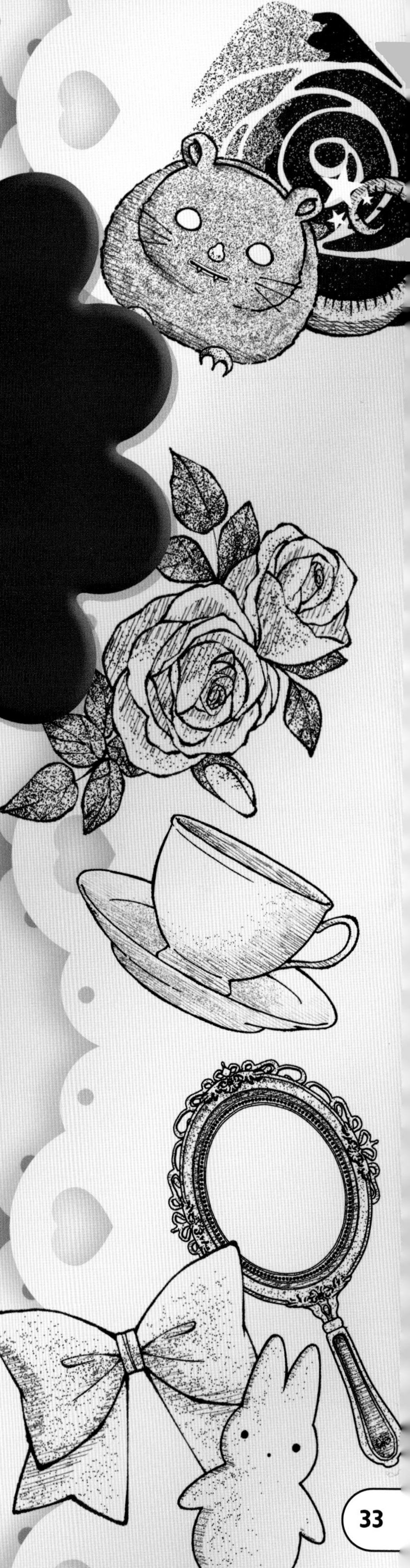

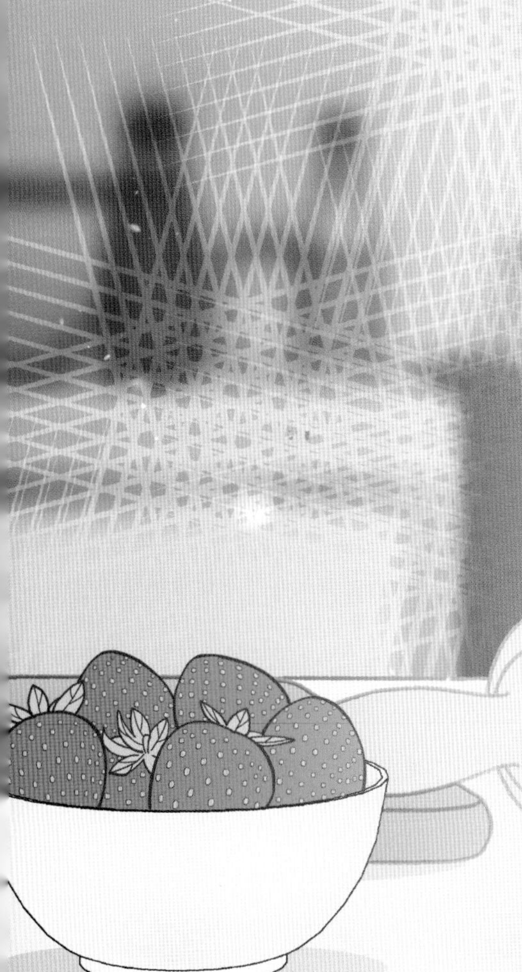

TOOLS & MATERIALS

Whether you are sketching on paper or drawing digitally, there are some basic tools that will help you on your artistic journey.

PENCILS

Graphite pencils come in various densities that help you achieve different shading techniques. The harder or denser the lead is, the lighter it will draw on paper. For a light shade, you can use a 2H pencil. An HB pencil will give you a medium shade, and for darker shades, you can use between 2B and 6B pencils. If you are a beginner artist, start with an HB pencil. Try different pencils and see which one works best for you.

ERASERS

When cleaning up your sketches, try using a good-quality rubber or vinyl eraser. You don't want something that will smudge your artwork as you are removing guidelines. A kneaded eraser is also a great tool and is a very pliable and versatile option that won't leave any dust or residue on your paper. You can mold the eraser into any shape to erase precisely.

PENS & INKS

Fine-line markers come in different widths and are easy to use. Once you have finalized your sketches, it is great to go back and finish with a clean, sharp line. Make sure to use permanent ink markers so they won't smudge when adding color or erasing pencil lines. If you want variety in your pen strokes, try using a brush pen. The more pressure you use with a brush pen, the thicker the lines. Light pressure is perfect for very fine details.

PAPER

A sketchbook is a great tool to always have handy when developing your art practice. They come in a variety of sizes and shapes. A good mixed-media sketchbook is a great place to start. If you are using paints or markers, choose a thicker paper so the wet media doesn't bleed through.

ADDING COLOR

Colored pencils are great for adding shading and depth to your drawings. Use sharp points for detail work. Markers are perfect for adding large areas of color. Apply your strokes in quick succession for a smooth, blended look. Let your strokes dry before building up layers of color. Watercolor paints are also great for coloring inked drawings.

DIGITAL TOOLS

Webcomics are created digitally, so it is great to familiarize yourself with digital drawing tools. There are many different drawing apps available at a low cost or even for free. Drawing tablets with pens can be used for digital drawing. There are many to choose from, so research and test out your options to find the right tablet for you.

I draw on an iPad Pro. I personally love drawing on it and think it feels the most similar to drawing with pen and paper, though I know that's not the same for everyone! I have it connected to my Mac using software called Astropad, which turns my iPad into a second computer screen I can draw on.

Most of the art is drawn, colored, and shaded in Clip Studio Paint, and the backgrounds are exported from a 3D modeling program called Sketchup. Then all the art gets assembled into a master file in Photoshop where I add the text bubbles and boxes and package it into a finished comic.

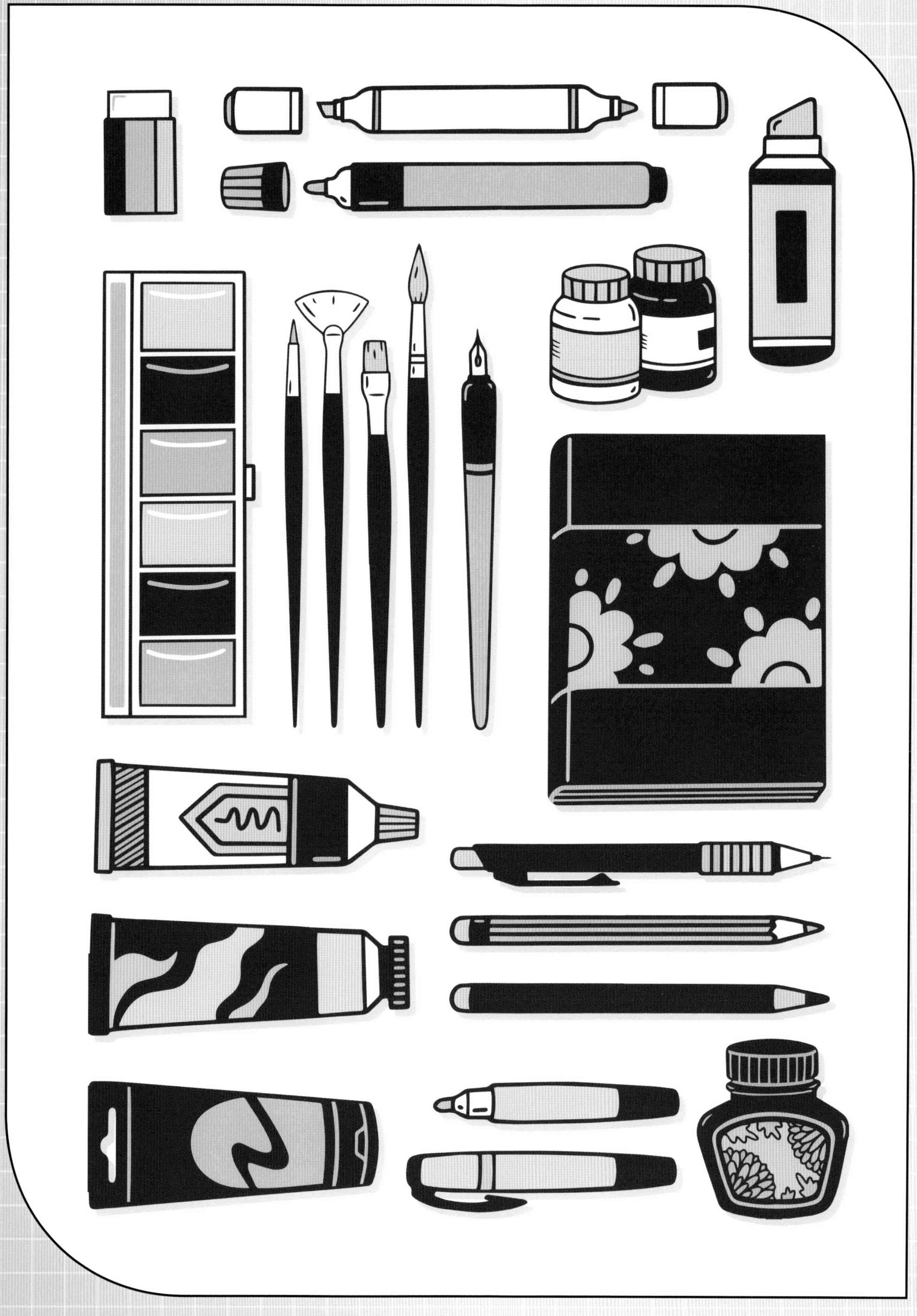

ANATOMY BASICS: THE HEAD

It's important to have a solid grasp of the basics when drawing people and characters. When you start to learn basic human anatomy and how it works, it is one of the easiest ways to learn how to draw a three-dimensional figure on a two-dimensional space.

FACE SHAPES & GUIDELINES

Begin each head with a simple circle; then sketch in the jaw and chin below it to create the face shape. When drawing a front view of the face, add a vertical guideline down the middle, and add a horizontal guideline across the face (halfway between the top of the head and the point of the chin). Notice how the face shape is determined by the size and angle of the jaw.

EYES & PROPORTIONS

Where the eyes sit on the face can vary between characters, but they usually fall somewhere on the horizontal guideline. Generally, the space between the eyes is about one eye's width, and the space between the outer corner of an eye and the edge of the head is about half an eye's width.

I give my characters a traditional manga flair with large eyes in relation to the head and other features.

FACIAL FEATURES

The placement and shapes of your characters' facial features are what make them unique. Notice Gwen's pointy ears, Syrah's (sometimes) long nose, and Blaine's red, almond-shaped eyes.

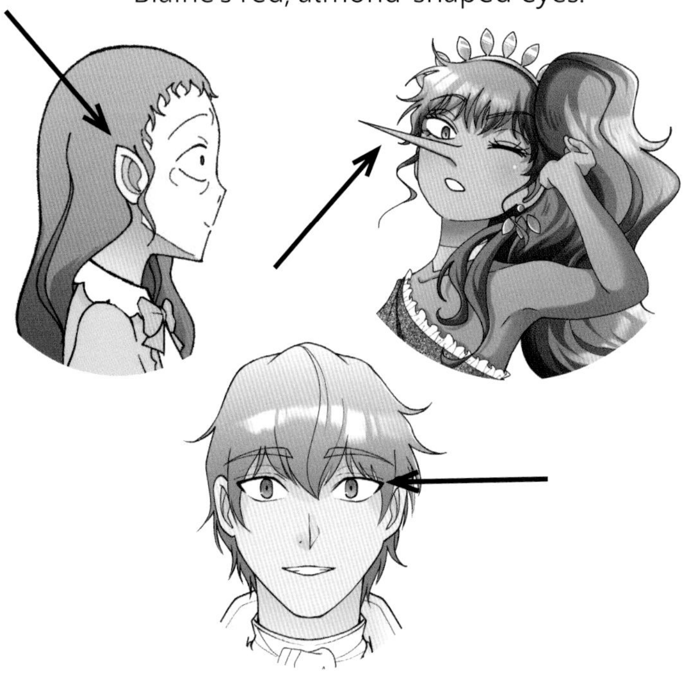

FACE VIEWS

There are three basic views of the face: the front view (A), the three-quarter view (B), and the profile or side view (C). When the head is kept level, the horizontal guidelines stay the same.

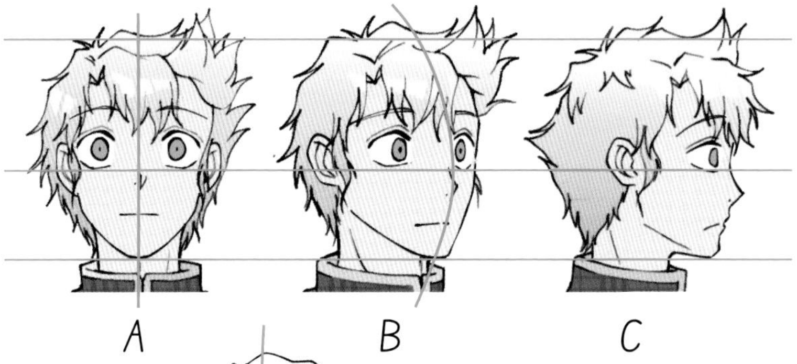

A
B
C

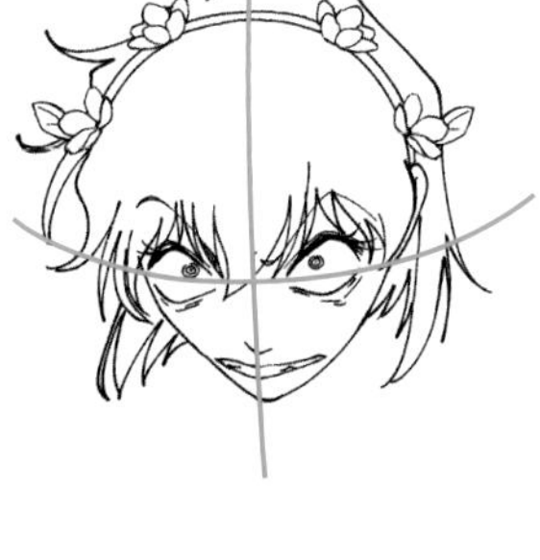

When the chin tilts up or down, the horizontal guidelines curve with the form of the head.

Here are some eye shapes among the characters of Cursed Princess Club.

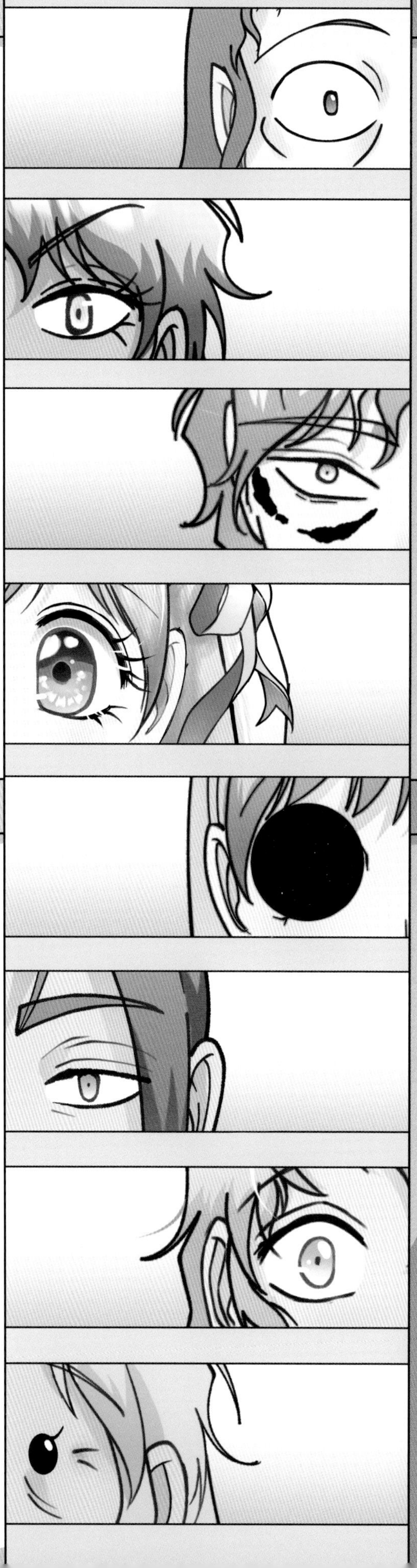

EXPRESSIONS & EMOTIONS

Expressions and emotions are important in webcomics because they help convey a character's mood and motivation, while contributing to the action and storyline of each scene.

Most expressions can be conveyed through the eyes and mouth. Wide eyes can express things like surprise, excitement, and shock. Open mouths can be shaped downward to convey alarm or anger, while upward-shaped mouths communicate excitement and joy.

Study the expressions on this spread and practice drawing a few of them. Mix and match different eye and mouth shapes to see what other expressions you can create.

HAPPY

SAD

ANGRY

ANNOYED

MENACING

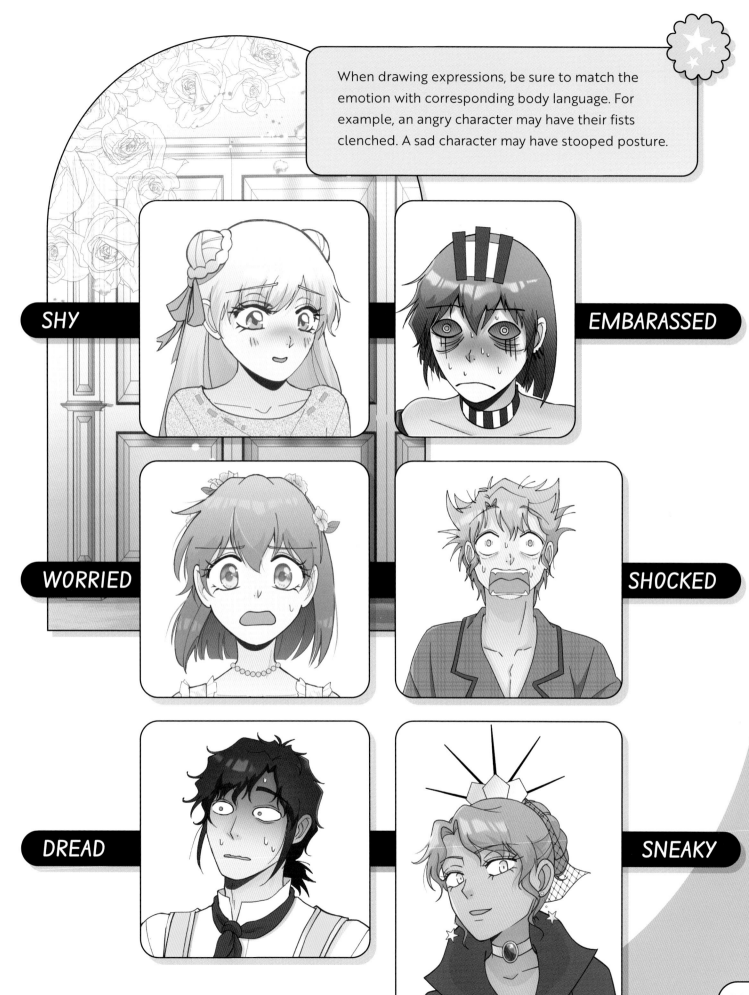

When drawing expressions, be sure to match the emotion with corresponding body language. For example, an angry character may have their fists clenched. A sad character may have stooped posture.

SHY

EMBARASSED

WORRIED

SHOCKED

DREAD

SNEAKY

ANATOMY BASICS: THE BODY

PROPORTIONS

One of the keys to drawing successful, believable bodies is to gain an understanding of basic human proportions (how the size of each body part relates to the whole body). However, think of these proportions as rough guidelines. Your characters' proportions should vary somewhat—this is what makes each of them unique and recognizable. At right, you can see Gwen's proportions. The horizontal blue lines help us see the most important markers for building her body, including her height, chin, shoulders, waist, knees, and bottoms of the feet.

For each character that you develop, it's a good idea to create a style sheet that showcases the body type, proportions, and unique features. You can reference this sheet as you build your series. However, you're not stuck with your original ideas; you're always free to refine your characters over time!

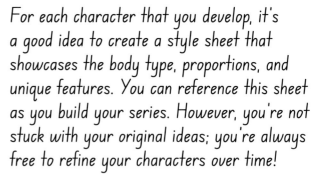

Mature females generally have wider hips and larger busts than males. Male bodies are often taller with broader shoulders, narrower hips, and thicker necks.

VIEWS OF THE BODY

Drawing characters requires a series of general steps as you work toward colored finals. Practice drawing figures from different angles to see how the guidelines and body shapes shift.

FRONT VIEW

Begin with a gestural sketch—a rough layout of the character's most basic lines and posture. Then block in the outer edges and ink in the form to complete the figure.

VIEW

In a 3/4 view, the character is turned slightly away from the viewer, which both obscures and exposes portions of the figure. Note that the vertical guideline of the face is curved.

PROFILE VIEW

The horizontal guidelines on a figure in profile are the same as a front or 3/4 view. However, note the angled guidelines of the face.

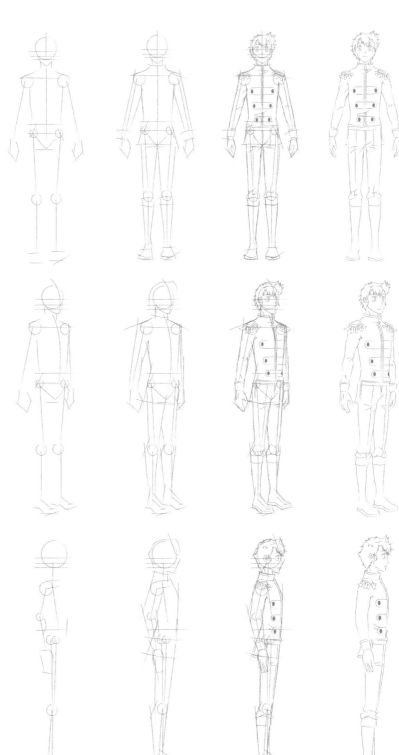

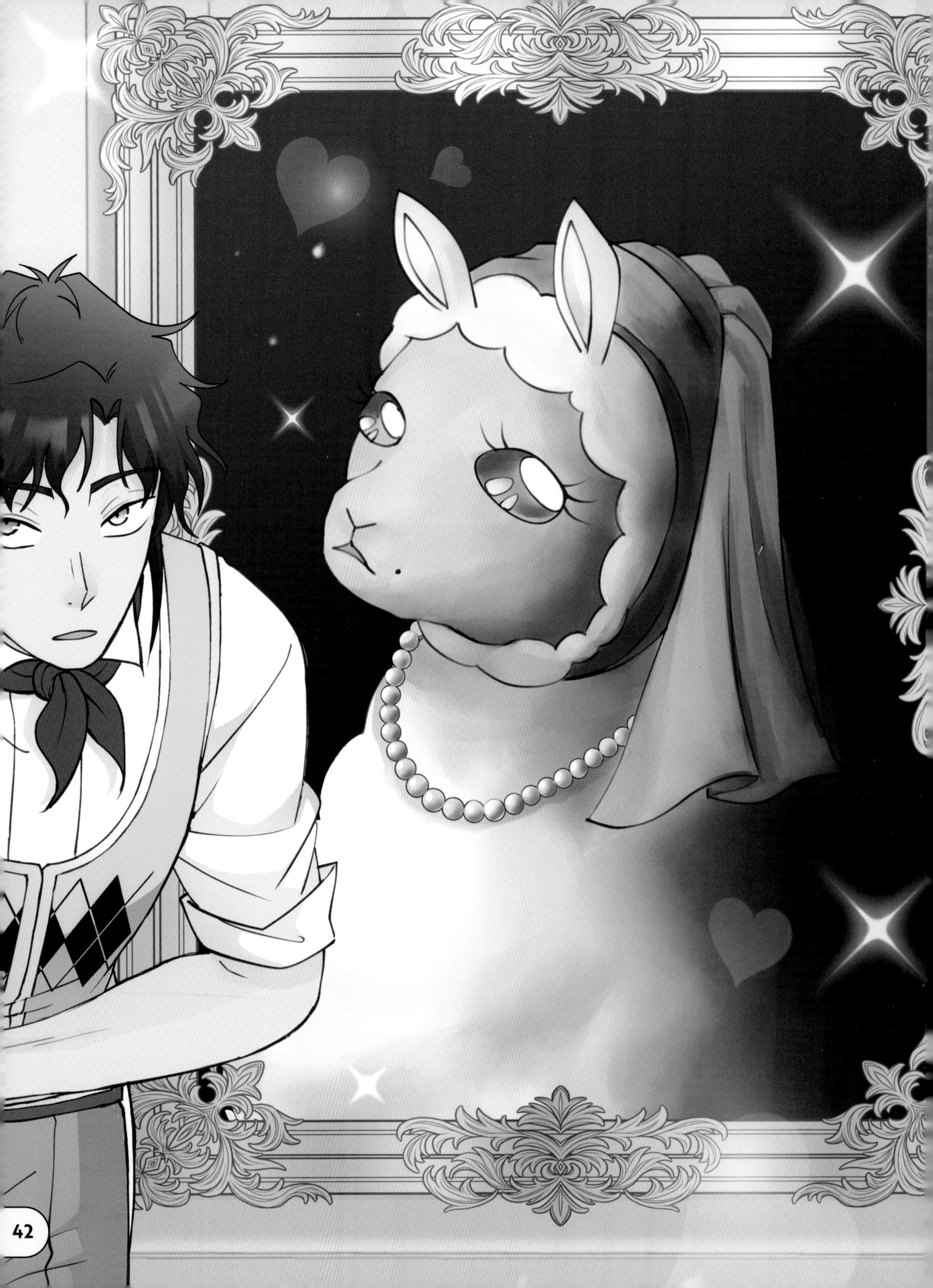

DRAWING STEP BY STEP

Learn to draw your favorite characters from Cursed Princess Club.

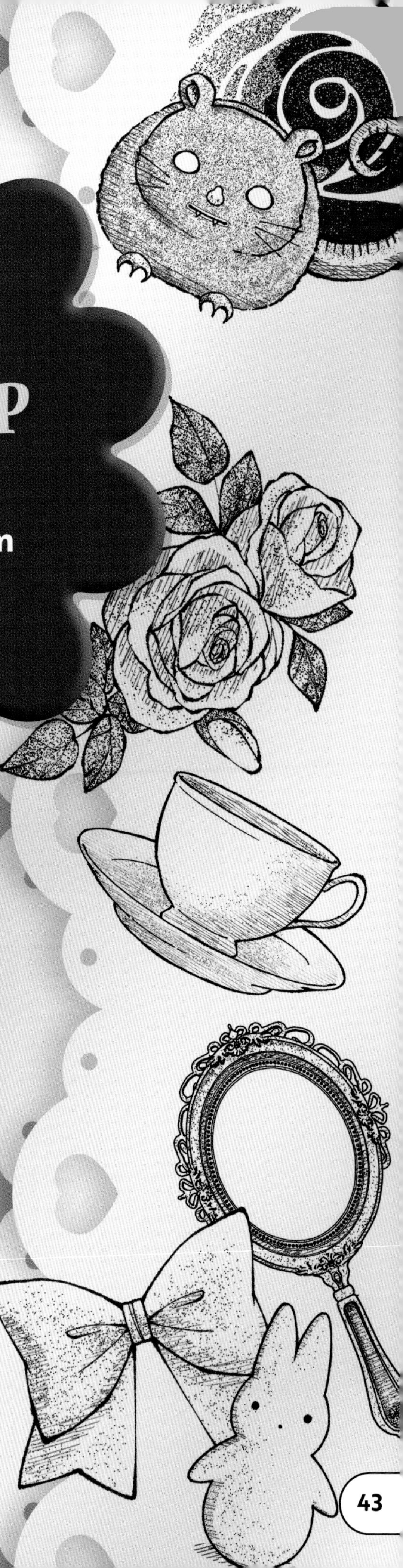

LEARN TO DRAW GWEN: HEAD

Gwen's kind and innocent nature is reflected in her wide eyes, arched eyebrows, and oval-shaped smile. She often has a look of surprise on her face, but her expressions range from looks of concern to sadness to wonder.

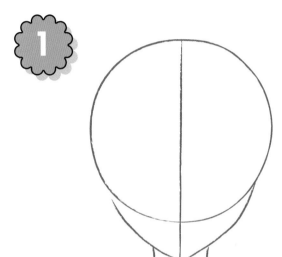

Gwen has protruding folds around her eyes, which appear as a few curved lines around her eye sockets.

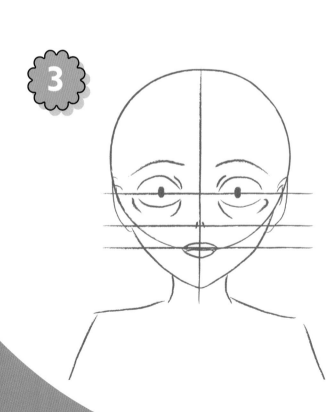

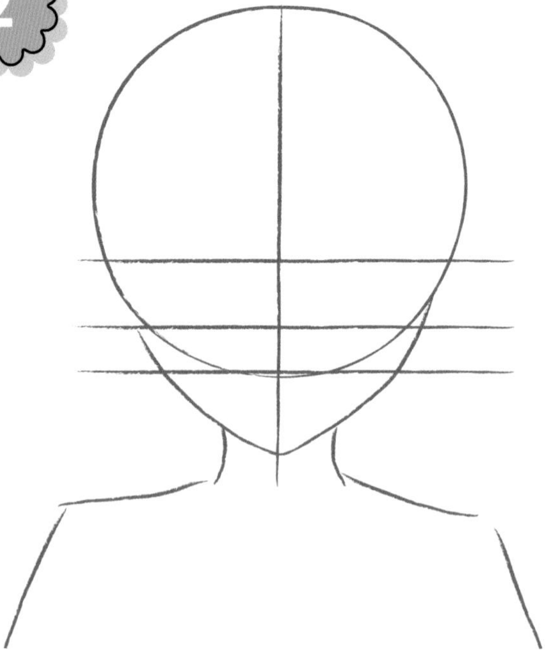

Start with the basic outline of the face; then add guidelines so you know where to place the features. Begin roughing in the eyes, nose, and mouth.

4

Continue to fine-tune the details and erase unnecessary sketch lines. Complete Gwen's outfit and add shading and any final touches before going to color.

5

6

Gwen has sharp fanged canines, and one or two sometimes peek out of her mouth. Her wavy hair is like limp seaweed.

LEARN TO DRAW GWEN: BODY

Gwen's body type is petite with bony features. She's drawn in a way that makes her always look a little awkward and uncoordinated, which matches her overall appearance and personality.

When showing a character in motion, make sure that their clothes appear to move in line with their body.

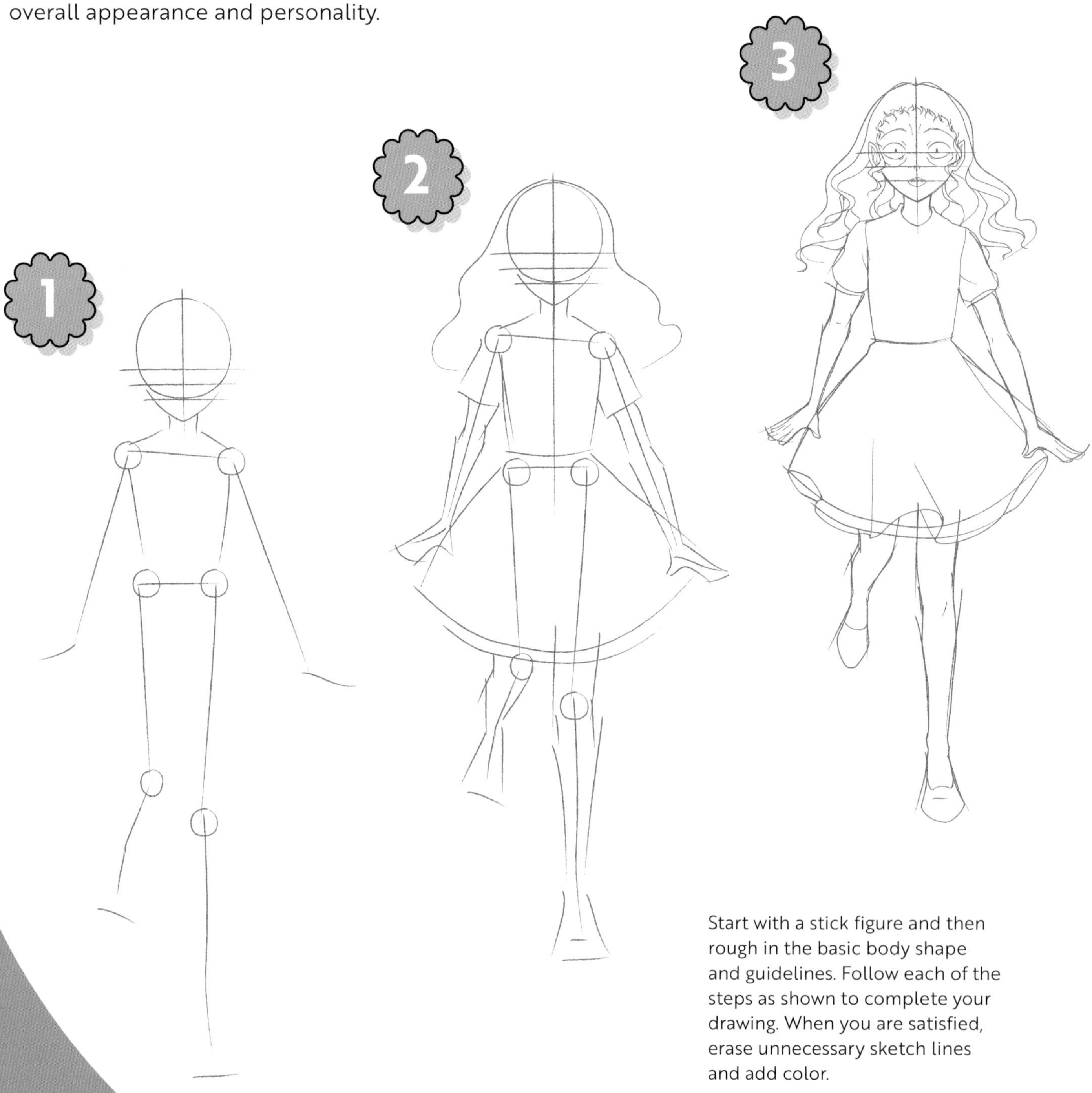
1
2
3

Start with a stick figure and then rough in the basic body shape and guidelines. Follow each of the steps as shown to complete your drawing. When you are satisfied, erase unnecessary sketch lines and add color.

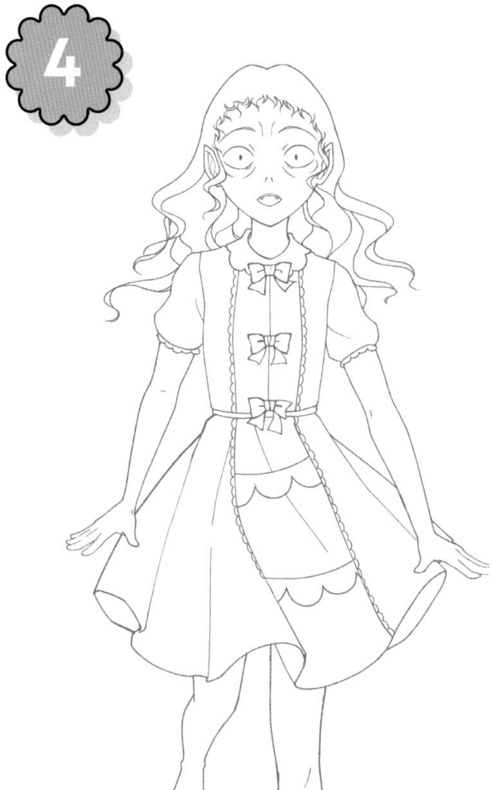
4

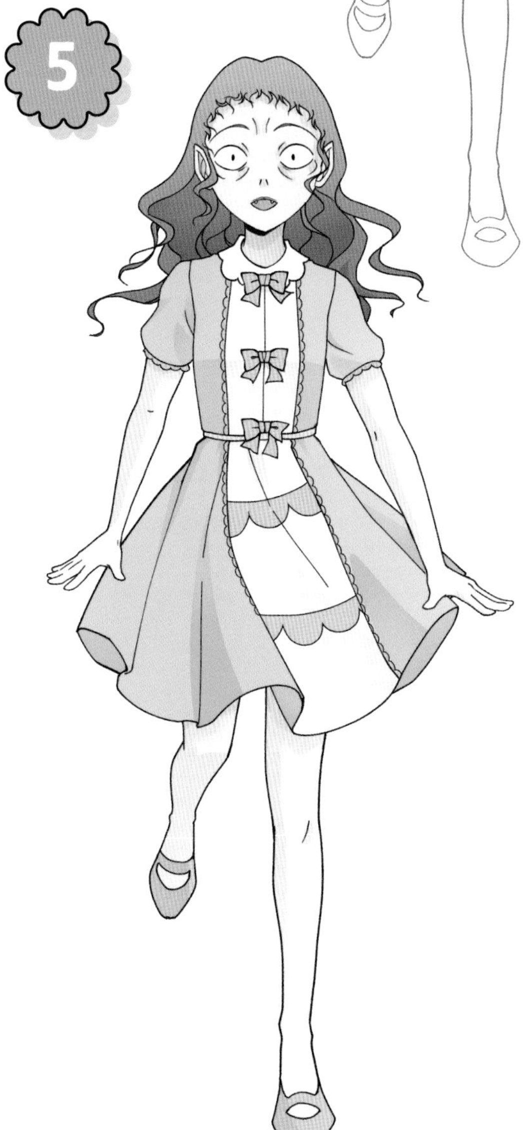
5

WARDROBE & STYLE

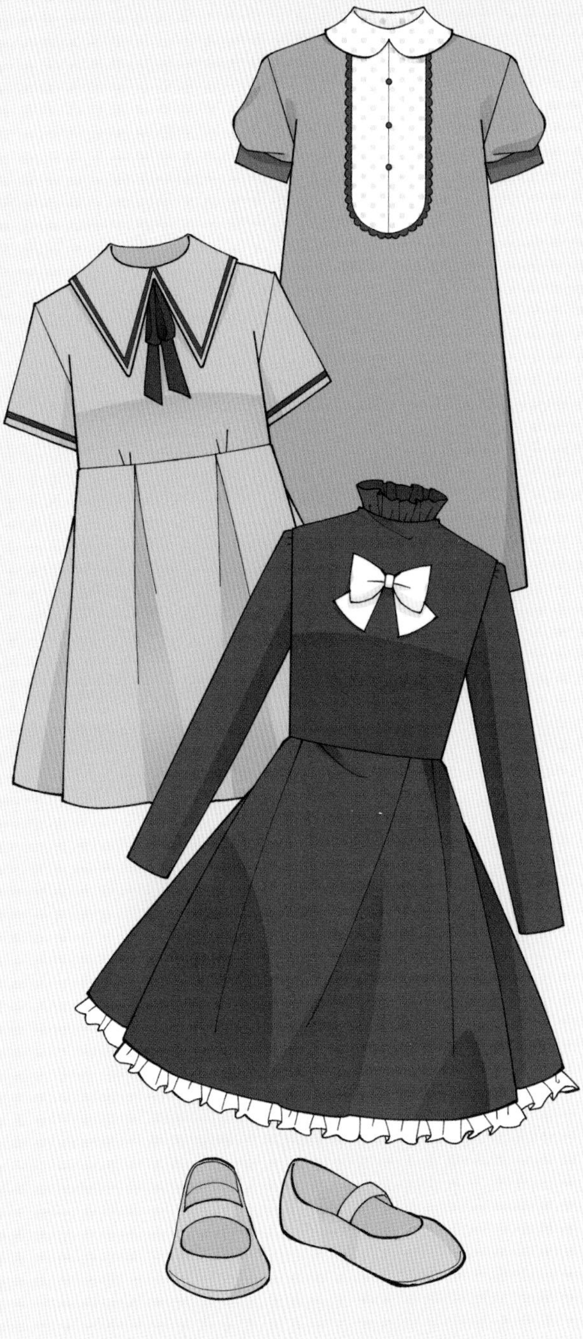

Gwen has an innocent, girly style that includes pleated and A-line dresses with Peter Pan, sailor, and ruffled collars. She wears flats and Mary Janes.

LEARN TO DRAW MARIA: HEAD

Maria is the Cinderella of the Pastel Kingdom. She's a classic beauty, whose sweet nature attracts woodland creatures to come forth and tend to her hair and clothing. Her signature color is blue. She wears a lot of ribbons and ruffly clothes.

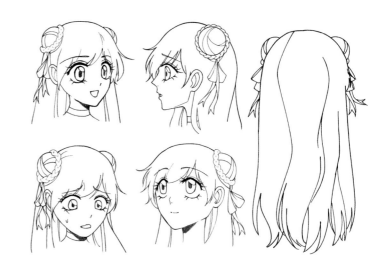

Maria's hair is soft and flowing. She often wears her long locks in braids tied with ribbons, which matches her romantic personality.

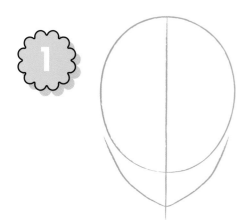

1

★ Maria's eyes are wide and always glimmering with curiosity.

2

3

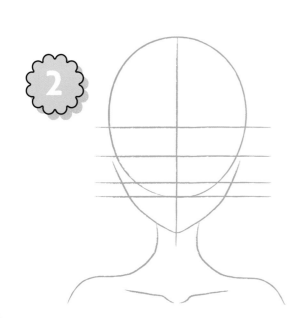
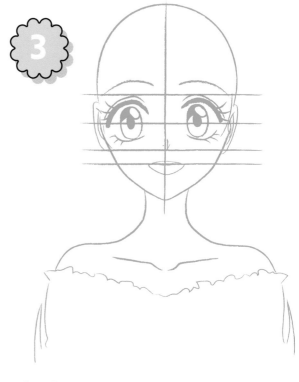

Start with the basic outline of the face; then add guidelines so you know where to place the features. Begin roughing in the eyes, nose, and mouth.

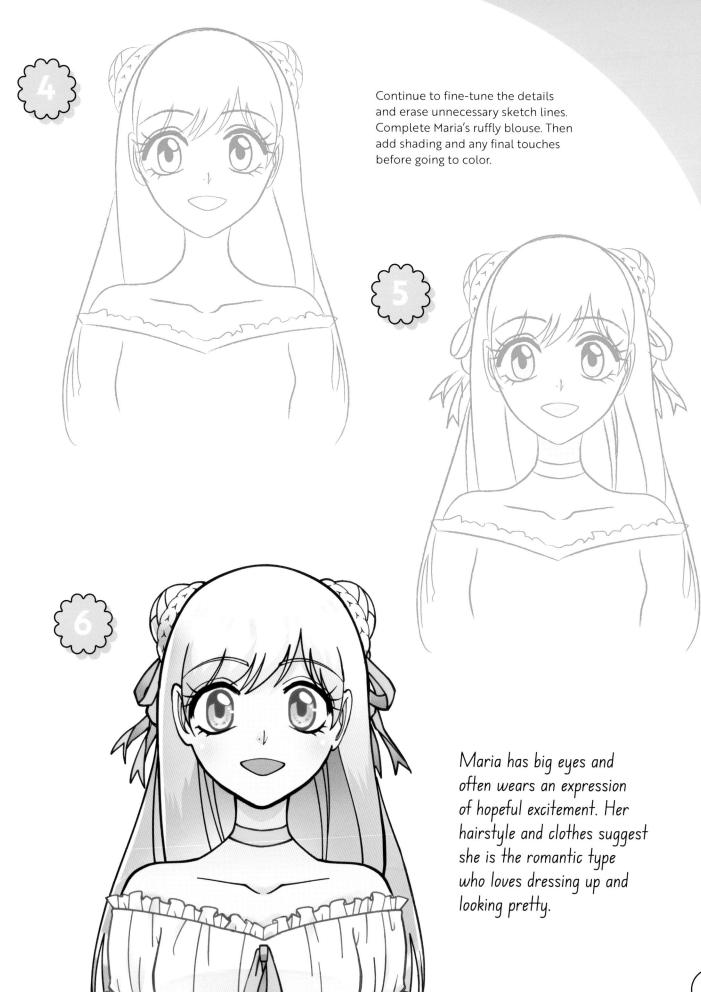

4

Continue to fine-tune the details and erase unnecessary sketch lines. Complete Maria's ruffly blouse. Then add shading and any final touches before going to color.

5

6

Maria has big eyes and often wears an expression of hopeful excitement. Her hairstyle and clothes suggest she is the romantic type who loves dressing up and looking pretty.

LEARN TO DRAW MARIA: BODY

Maria is a little more poised than Gwen. She is confident in herself, and it comes across in her posture and mannerisms when she's interacting with others. When drawing Maria's body, her position should look relaxed but refined.

Maria's hair is definitely her thing. She has signature braided buns and long, shiny hair that flows down her back.

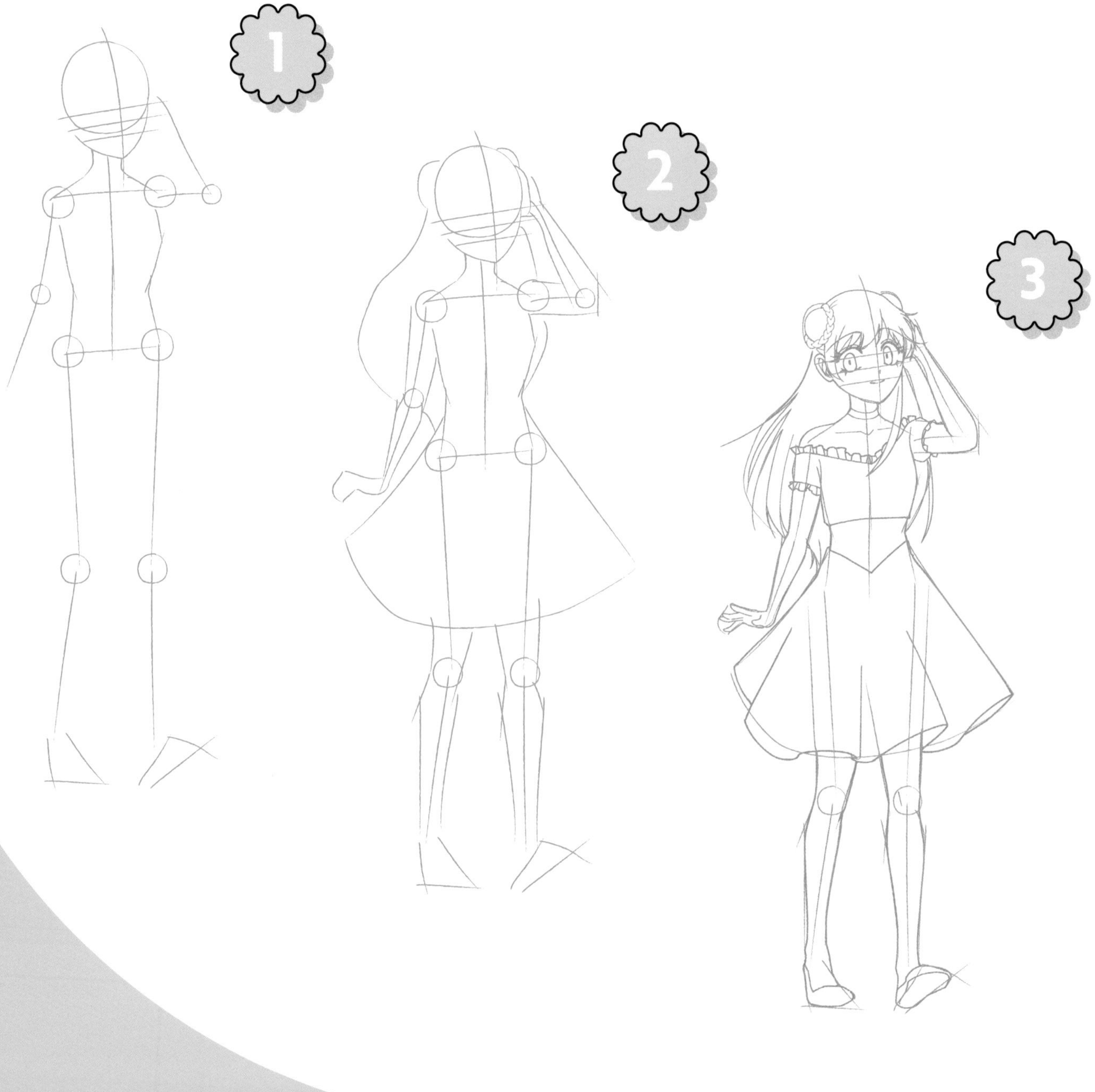
1
2
3

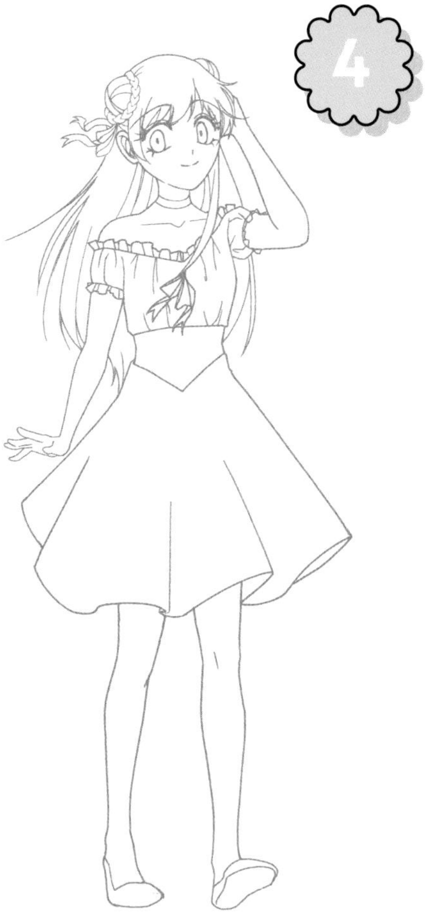
4

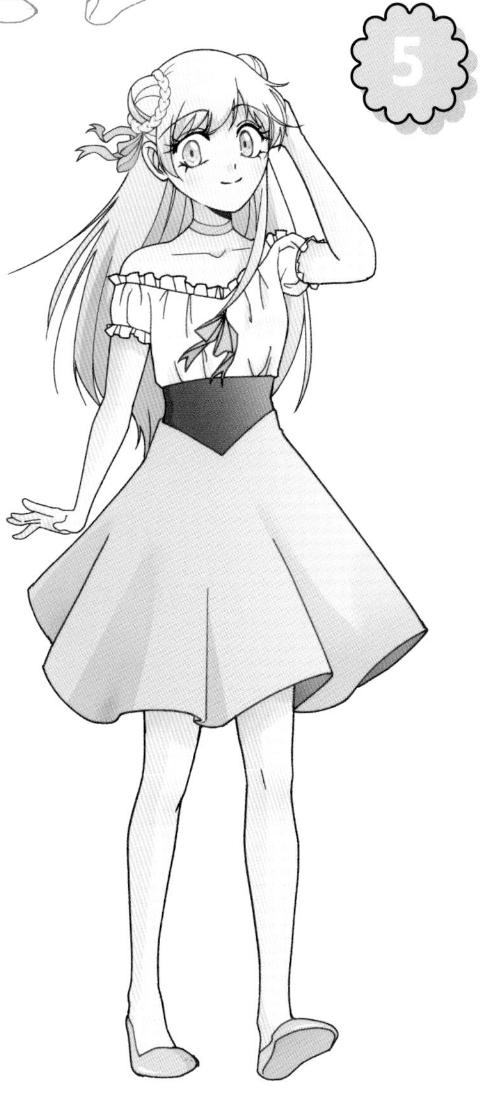
5

WARDROBE & STYLE

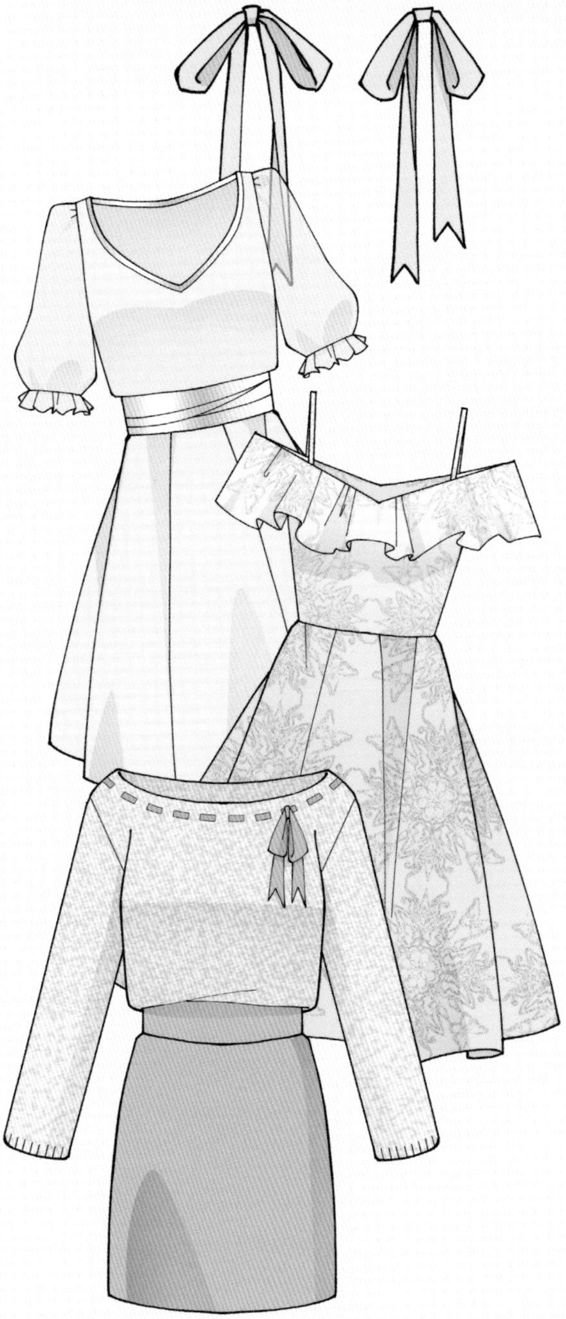

Maria wears dresses with a lot of frills, ruffles, and ribbons, as well as scoop-neck and off-the-shoulder blouses. Blue is her favorite color, which matches her sparkly eyes.

LEARN TO DRAW LORENA: HEAD

Lorena, like her sister, is such a beauty—even the flowers gravitate toward her. Lorena's color is lavender combined with soft shades of pink. You'll never go wrong adding flowers to her clothes, hair, or immediate surroundings.

1

A loving and loyal sister, Lorena says what's on her mind and is fiercely protective of her siblings. She wears a range of expressions from excitement to frustration.

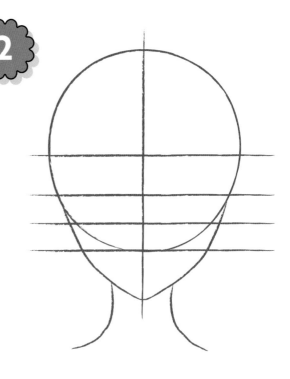

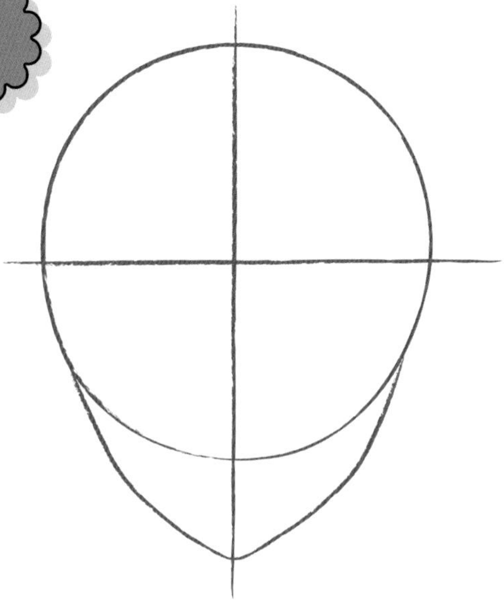

2

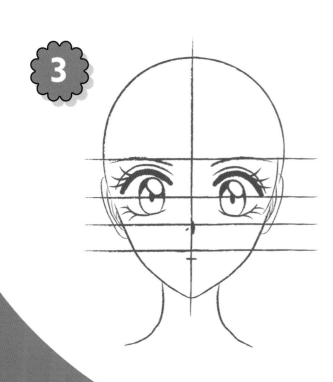

3

Start with the basic outline of the face; then add guidelines so you know where to place the features. Begin roughing in the eyes, nose, and mouth.

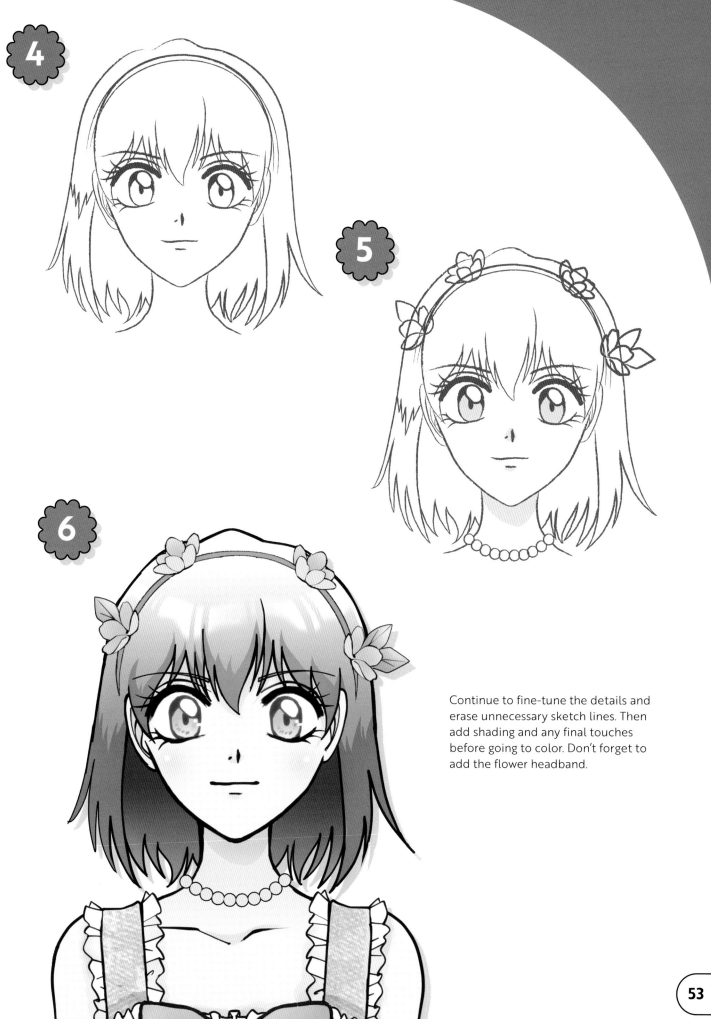

Continue to fine-tune the details and erase unnecessary sketch lines. Then add shading and any final touches before going to color. Don't forget to add the flower headband.

LEARN TO DRAW LORENA: BODY

Lorena is confident in herself and her athleticism, and this shows in her body position and posture. She is roughly the same height and body type as Maria.

Lorena's cute bob haircut matches her fun and fearless personality. Her bangs are layered and fall easily over her forehead.

1

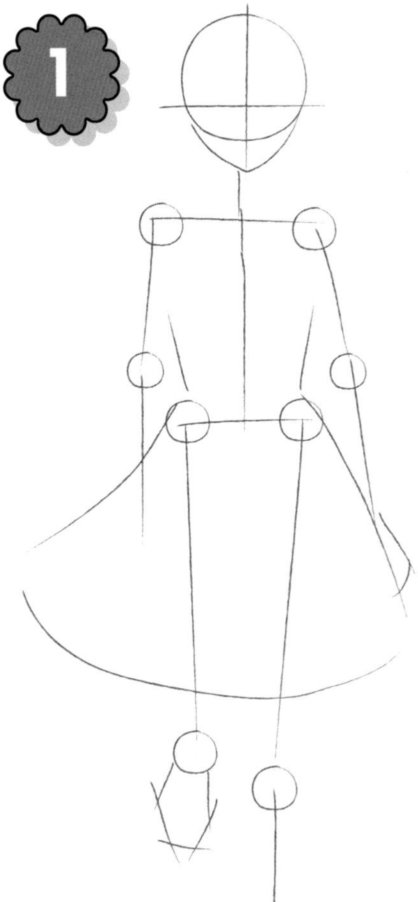

2

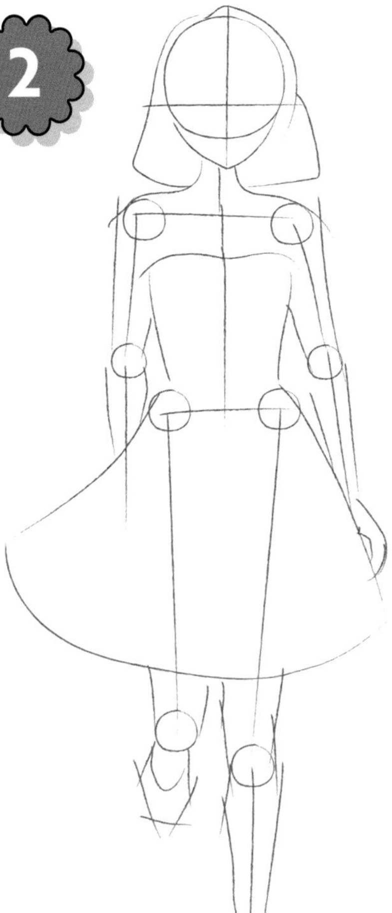

3

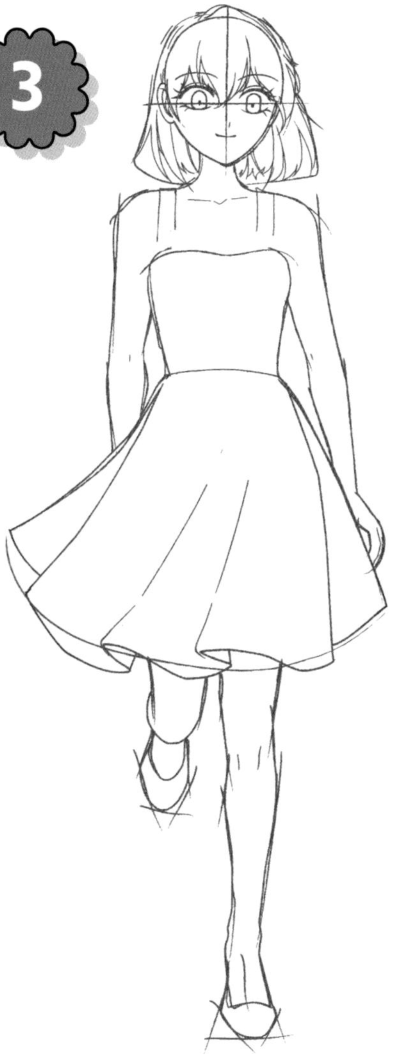

4

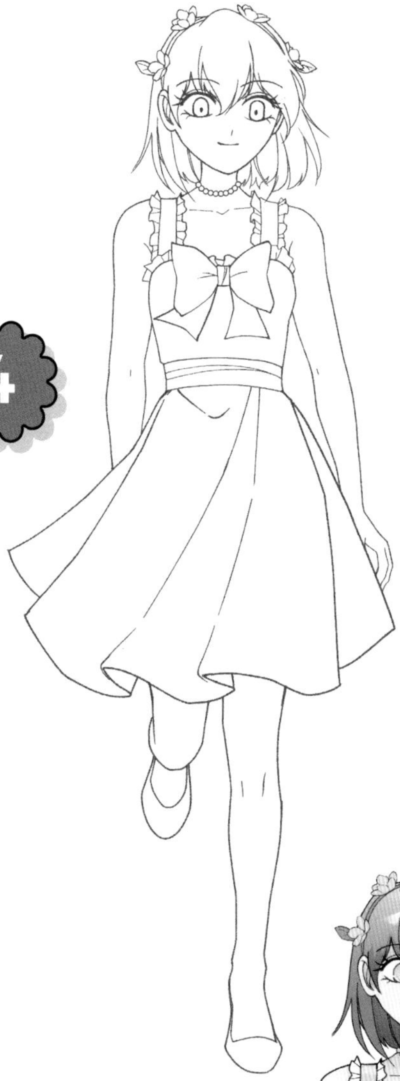

5

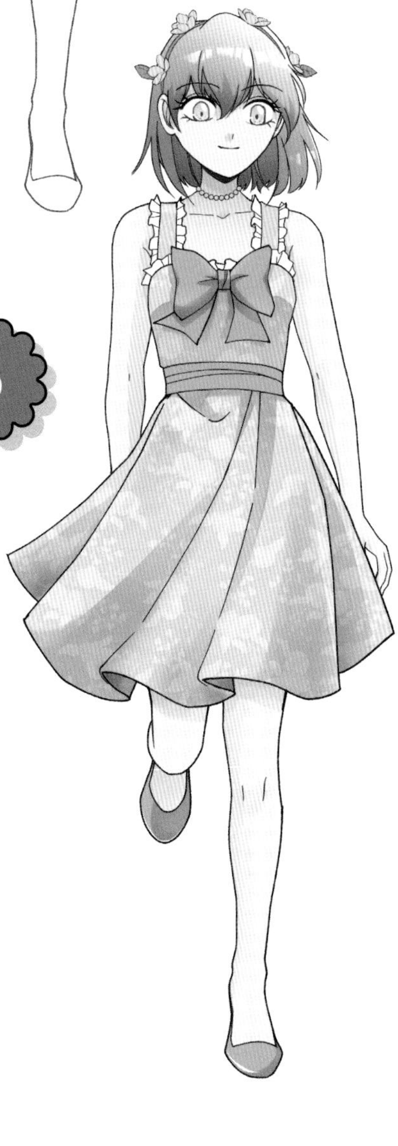

WARDROBE & STYLE

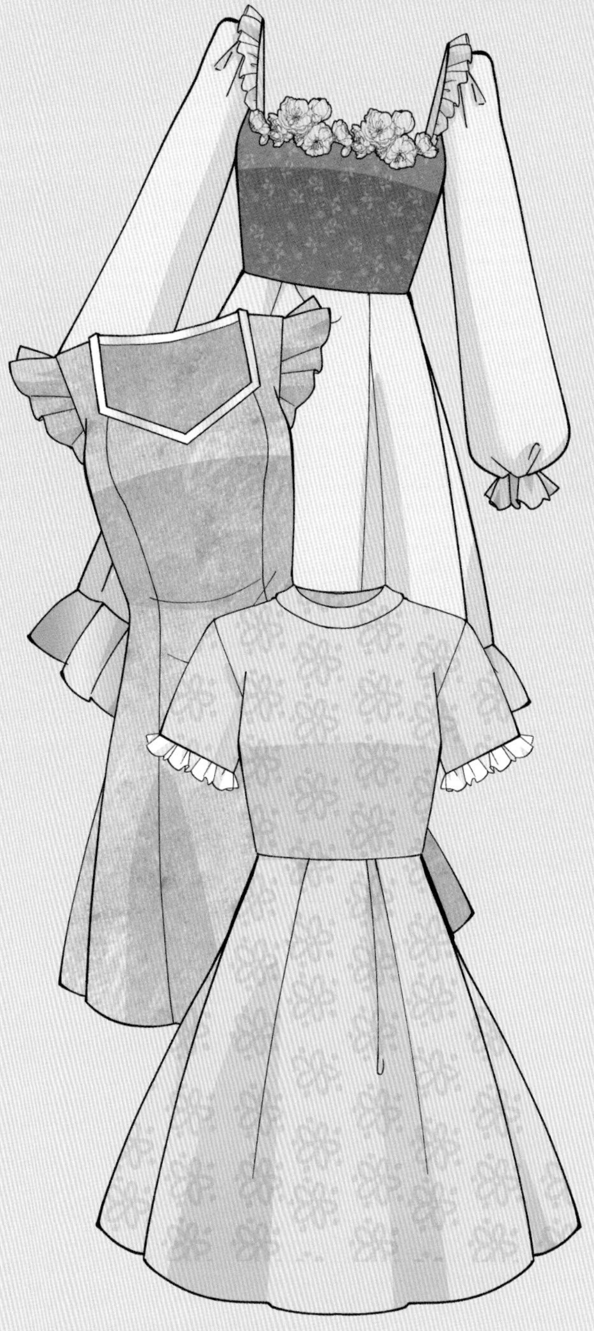

Purple is Lorena's go-to color, which she intersperses with various shades of pink and champagne. She loves one-piece dresses with floral patterns and designs.

LEARN TO DRAW JAMIE: HEAD

This three-quarter head pose shows Jamie's eyes looking slightly upward with a look of curiosity. Adding guidelines to your drawing will help you place the features in proportion.

Jamie's expressions can range from mischievous and surprised to sweet and happy. His hair, while stylish, is always slightly disheveled.

Jamie has a magical quality, so he is often surrounded by sparkles. The highlights in his eyes make them shimmer.

Start with the basic outline of the face. Notice the chin is pointed at a slight angle and only one ear is visible. Add the facial guidelines so you know where to place the features. Begin roughing in the eyes, nose, and mouth.

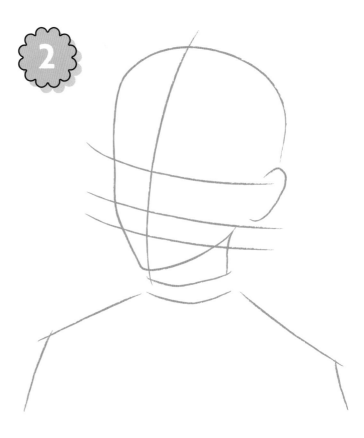

3

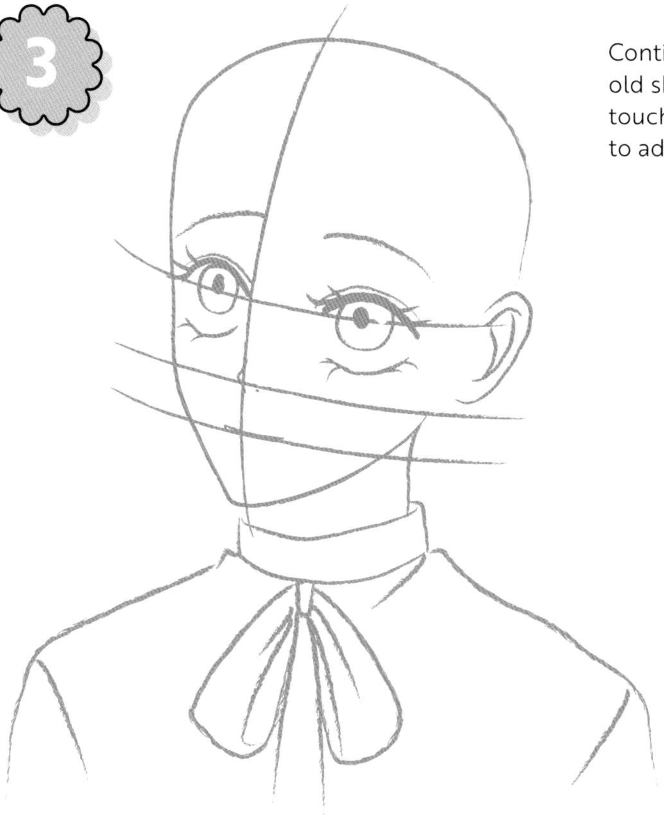

Continue to finesse the details and erase old sketch lines. Add shading and any final touches before going to color. Don't forget to add highlights to Jamie's hair and eyes.

4

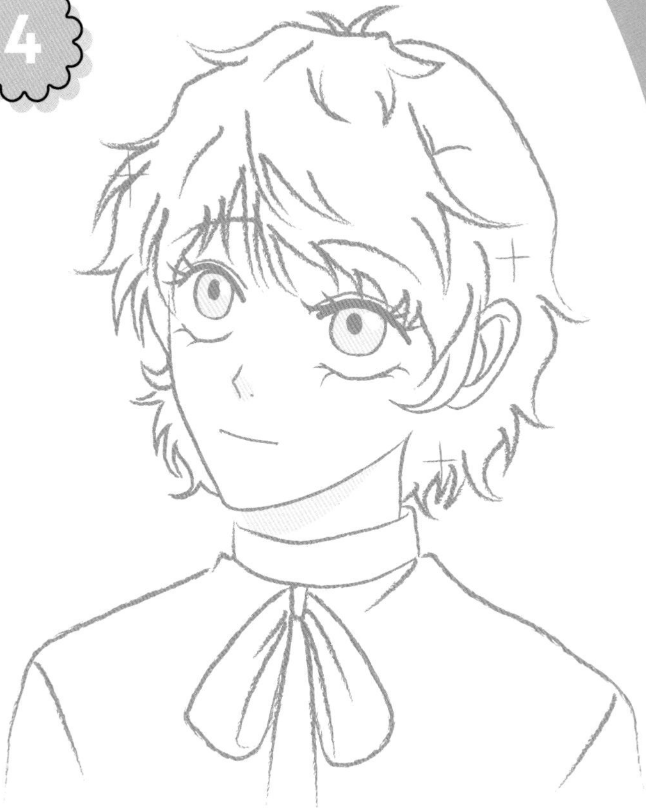

5

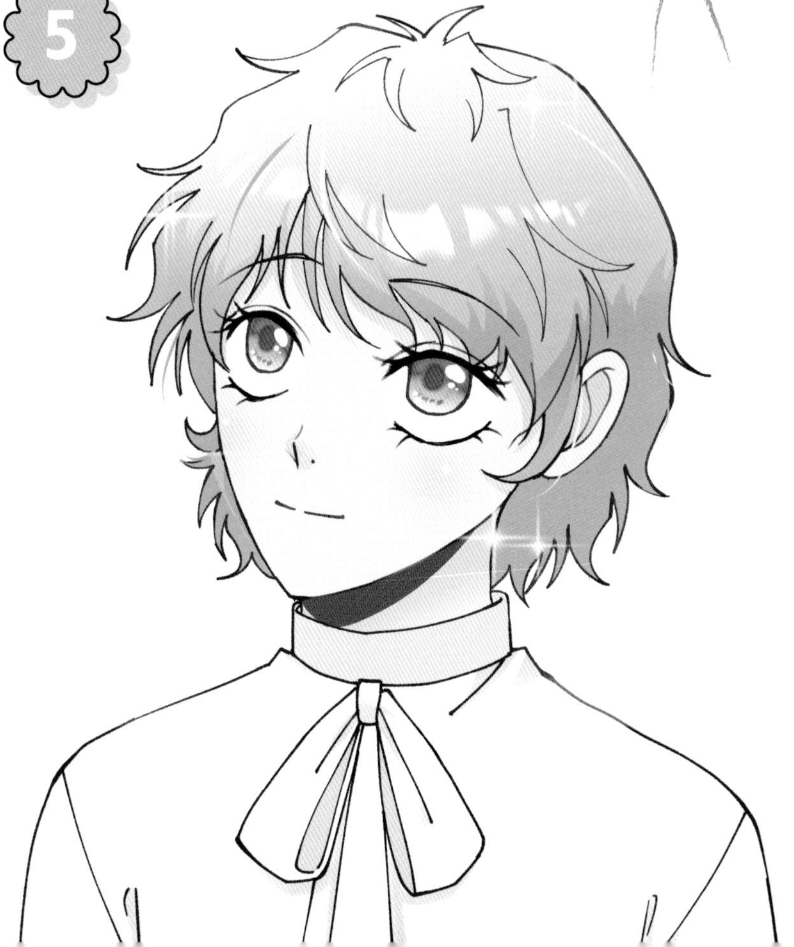

Jamie is pretty in pink, with beautiful shiny hair and bright lavender eyes. He has pieces of hair by his ears that curl toward his face.

LEARN TO DRAW JAMIE: BODY

Jamie has a laidback, carefree quality about him, so he is often in positions that suggest a relaxed state of being. In this pose, he is leaning back. It may look challenging, but just follow the steps. Don't forget to add highlights to his hair and sparkles around his body!

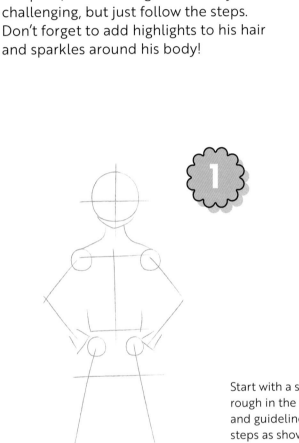

Start with a stick figure and then rough in the basic body shape and guidelines. Follow each of the steps as shown to complete your drawing. When you are satisfied, erase unnecessary sketch lines and add color.

4

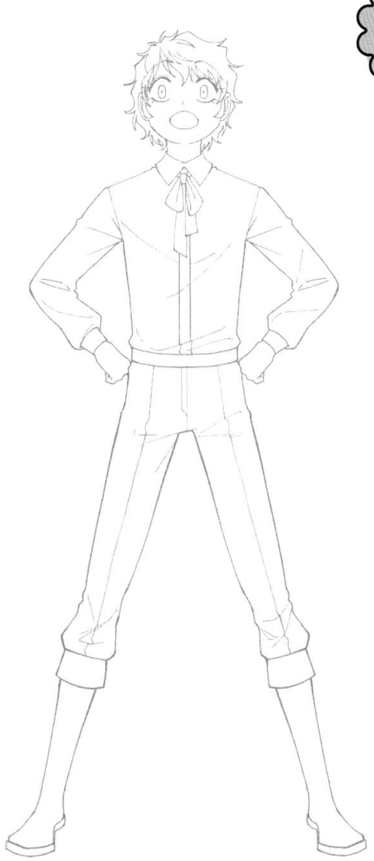

5

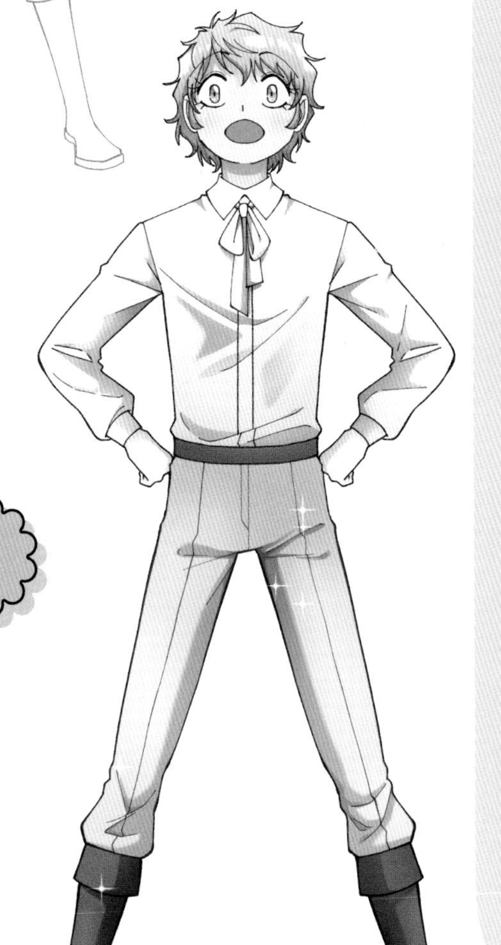

WARDROBE & STYLE

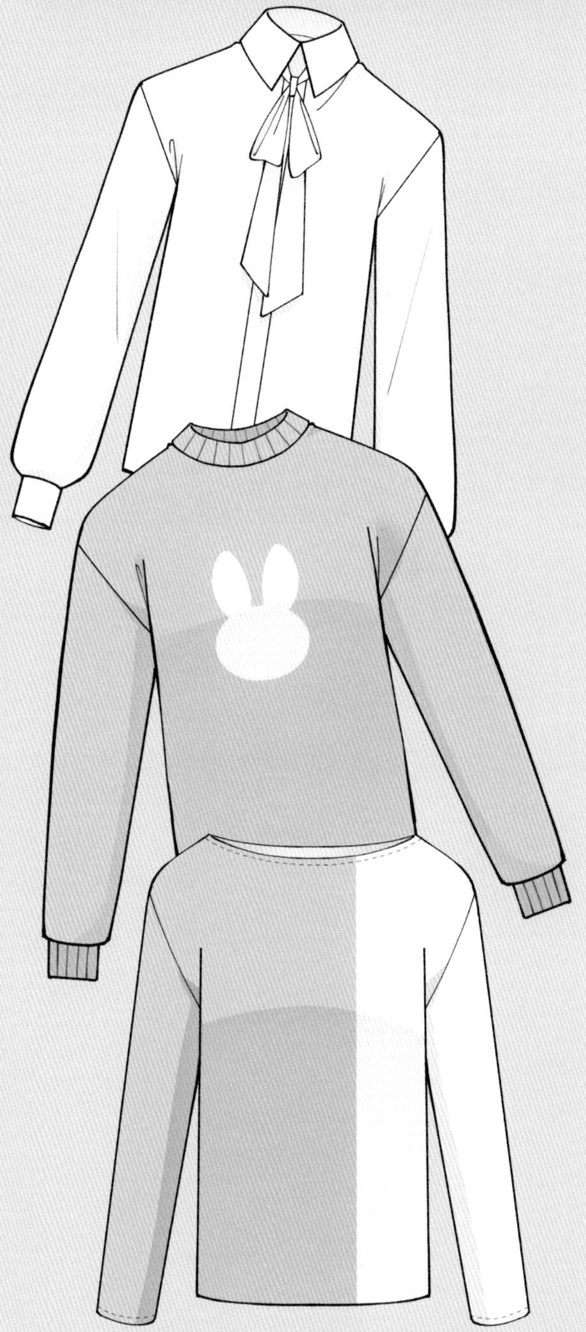

Jamie enjoys a casual, whimsical style that matches his unfettered, free-spirited personality. He's a fan of pink, which matches his hair.

LEARN TO DRAW FREDERICK: HEAD

Frederick has wide eyes but rather small eyeballs, which help communicate his generally anxious personality. Sometimes beads of sweat form on his face when he's feeling especially uneasy.

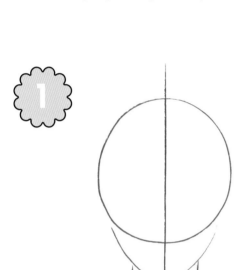

Frederick shows a lot of different emotions throughout the series, especially when he is feeling conflicted about Gwen.

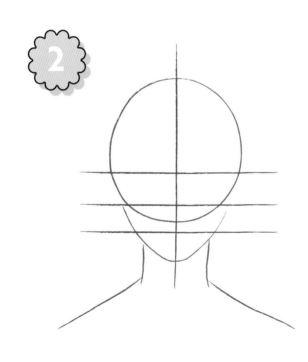

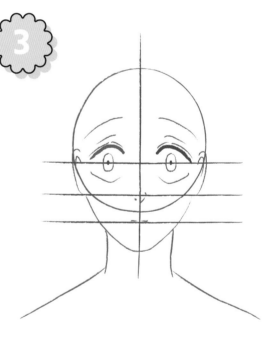

Start with the basic outline of the face; then add guidelines so you know where to place the features. Begin roughing in the eyes, nose, and mouth.

4

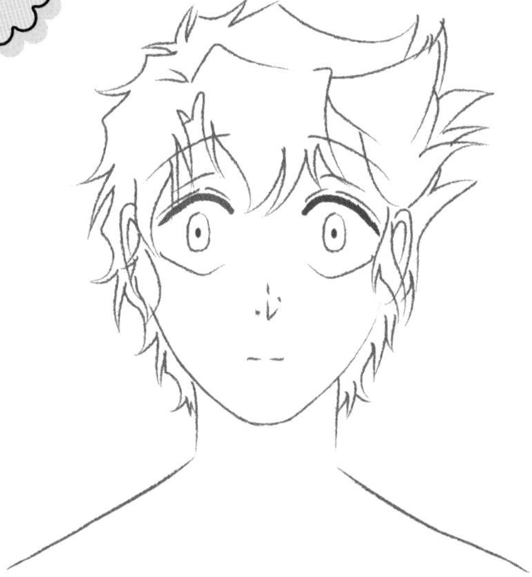

5

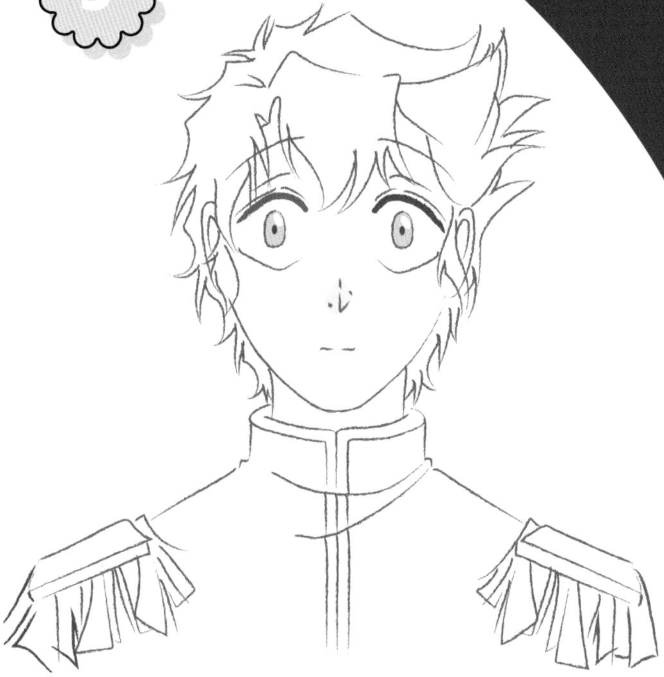

Continue to add the details and erase unnecessary sketch lines before adding color. Don't forget to add highlights to Frederick's hair and jacket.

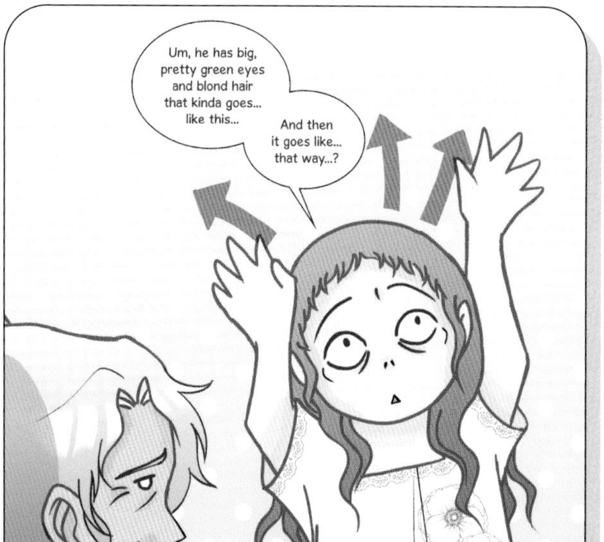
Um, he has big, pretty green eyes and blond hair that kinda goes... like this...
And then it goes like... that way...?
...what?...

6

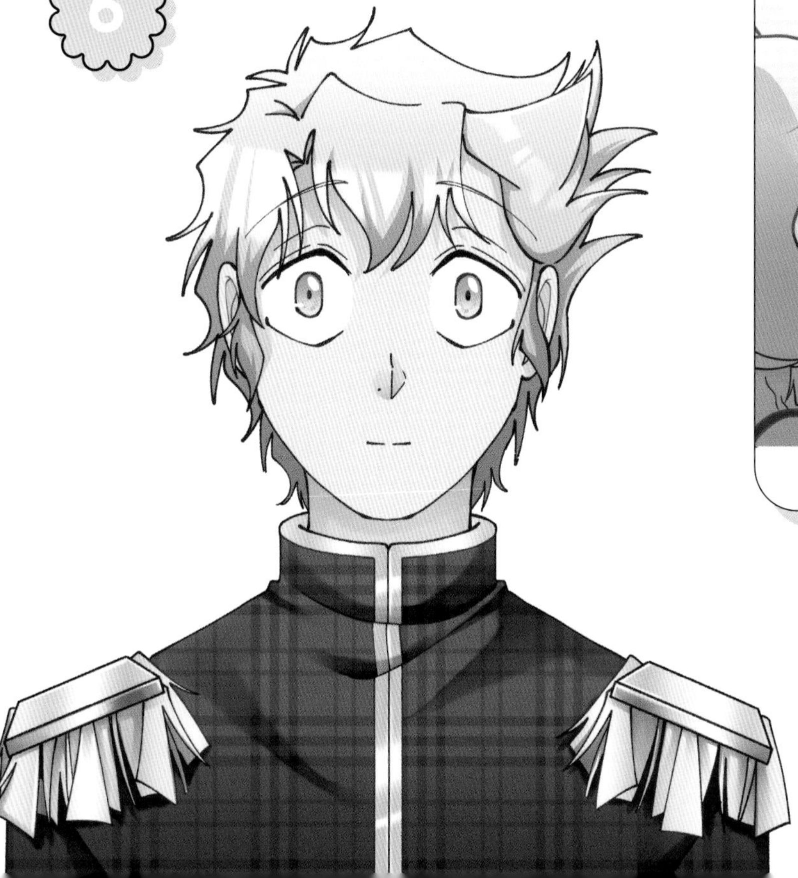

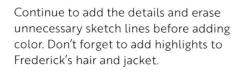

Frederick has a unique, asymmetrical hairstyle that Abbi refers to as "a broom that dried at a weird angle."

LEARN TO DRAW
FREDERICK: BODY

In many ways, Frederick is like his brothers, although not as big, strong, charismatic, or put together. His anxious personality often has him positioned in a way that suggests he's less than confident—especially around Gwen.

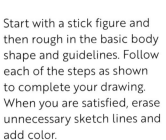

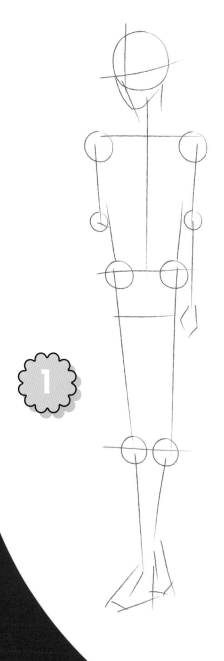

Start with a stick figure and then rough in the basic body shape and guidelines. Follow each of the steps as shown to complete your drawing. When you are satisfied, erase unnecessary sketch lines and add color.

Frederick wears his heart on his sleeve, and it often shows in his body language. With one arm clasped behind his back, this pose suggests he's feeling insecure and awkward.

4

5

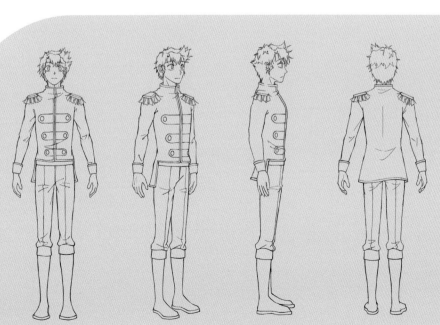

When learning how to draw full-body poses, it's helpful to practice drawing the body from a variety of different angles.

63

LEARN TO DRAW BLAINE: HEAD

Blaine has a pointed, slightly rounded jaw. His eyes tilt up at the outer corners and his hair is generally neat.

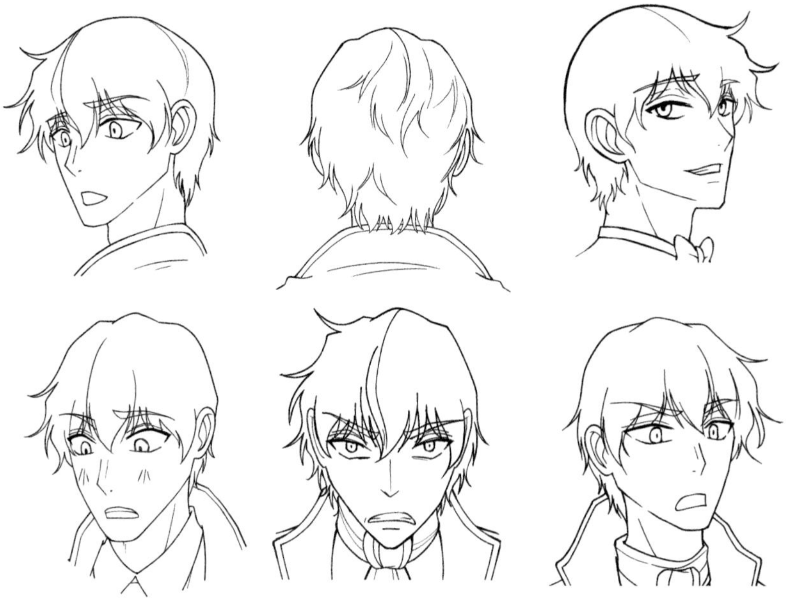

Notice how Blaine and Lance's hairstyles look slightly different when they're drawn at different angles.

1

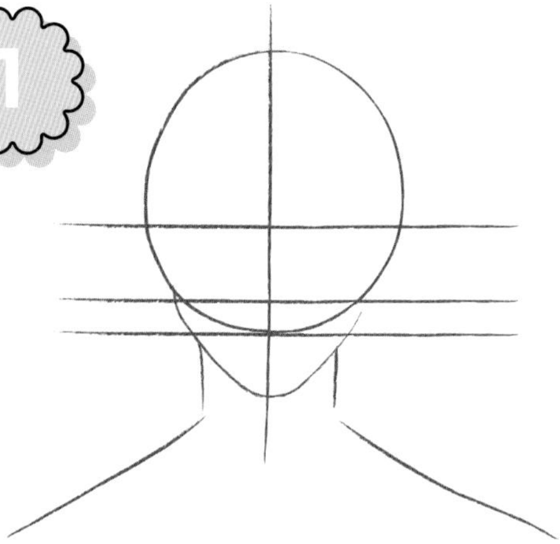

2

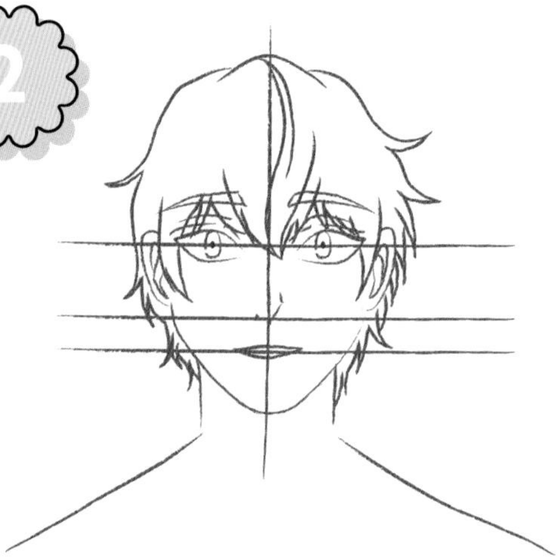

3

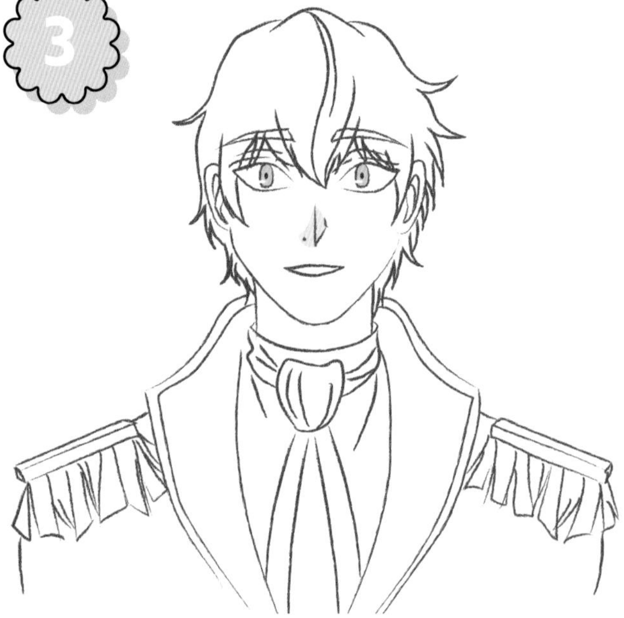

4

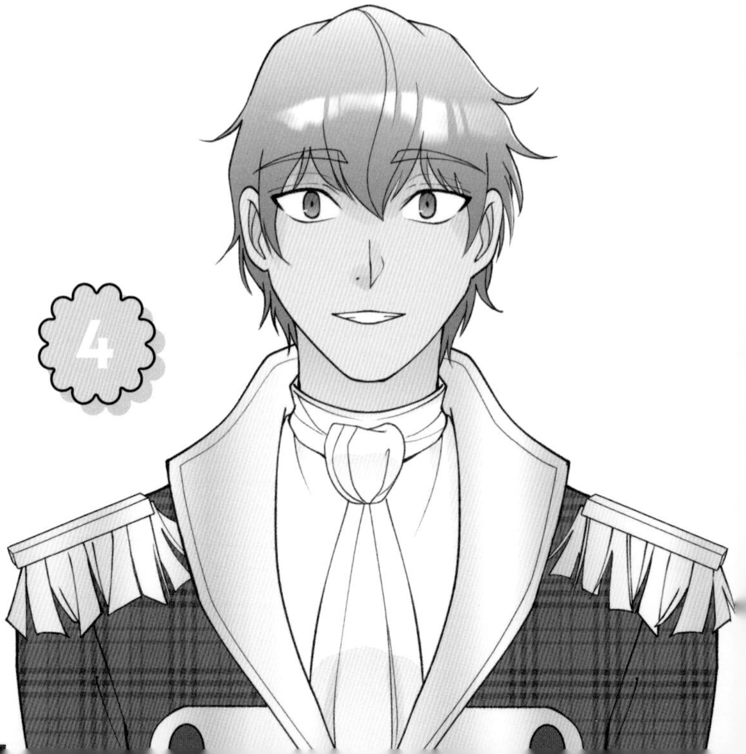

LEARN TO DRAW LANCE: HEAD

Lance has a more angular jawline than Blaine and a more muscular neck. His eyes gently slope down at the outer corners. His hair is cut short with choppy edges.

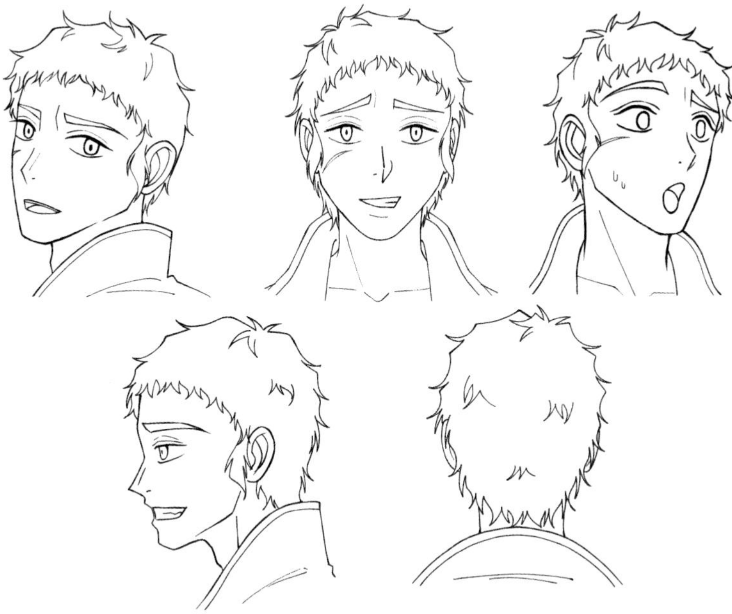

1

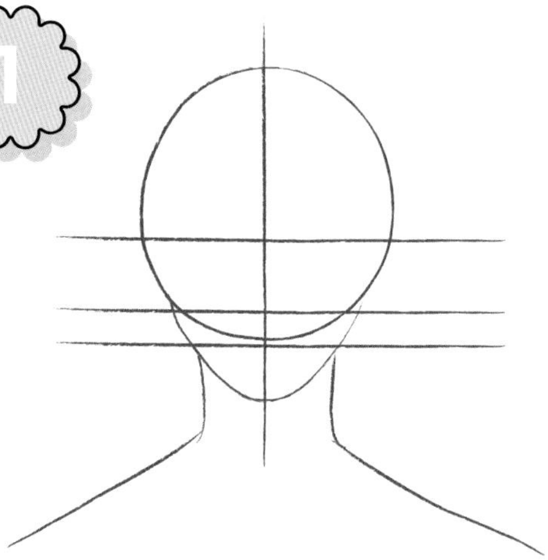

2

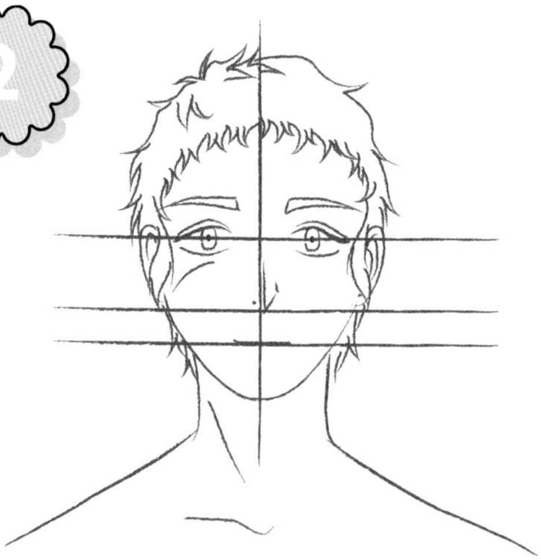

3

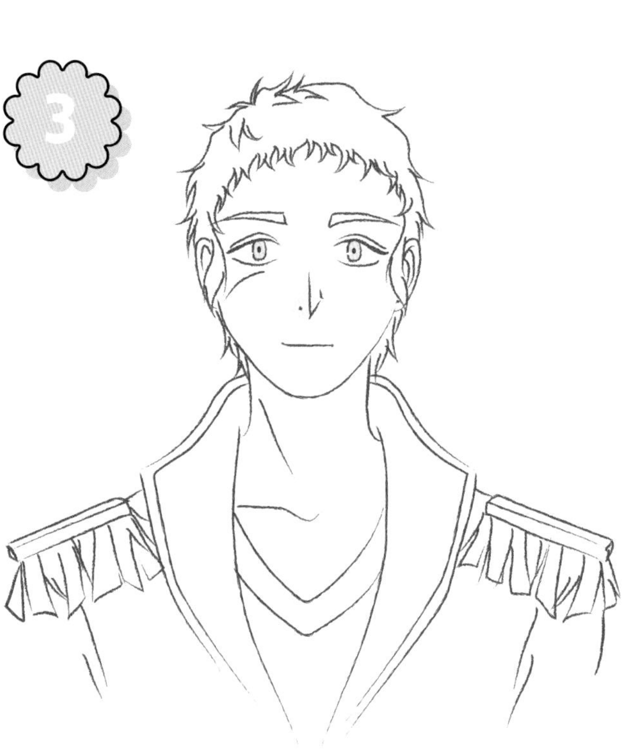

4

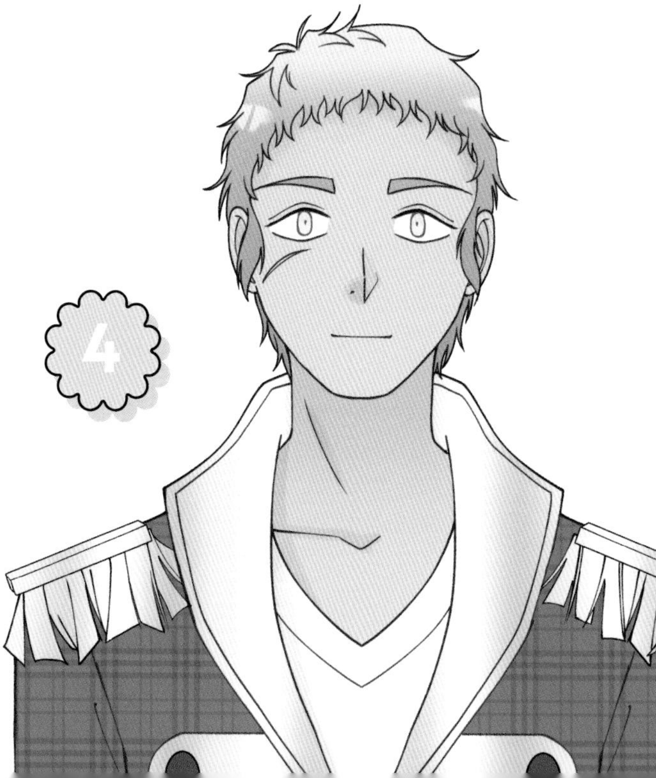

LEARN TO DRAW LANCE: BODY

Lance and Blaine share similar body types. Frederick is similar to his brothers in shape, though smaller. So once you master drawing one of them, you'll be able to draw all of them with minor adjustments.

Lance's V-neck T-shirt always looks slightly unkempt or informal.

Rough in the shape of Lance; then continue to fill in the details. When you are satisfied with your drawing, erase any unnecessary sketch lines and then color your drawing. Try drawing Blaine next!

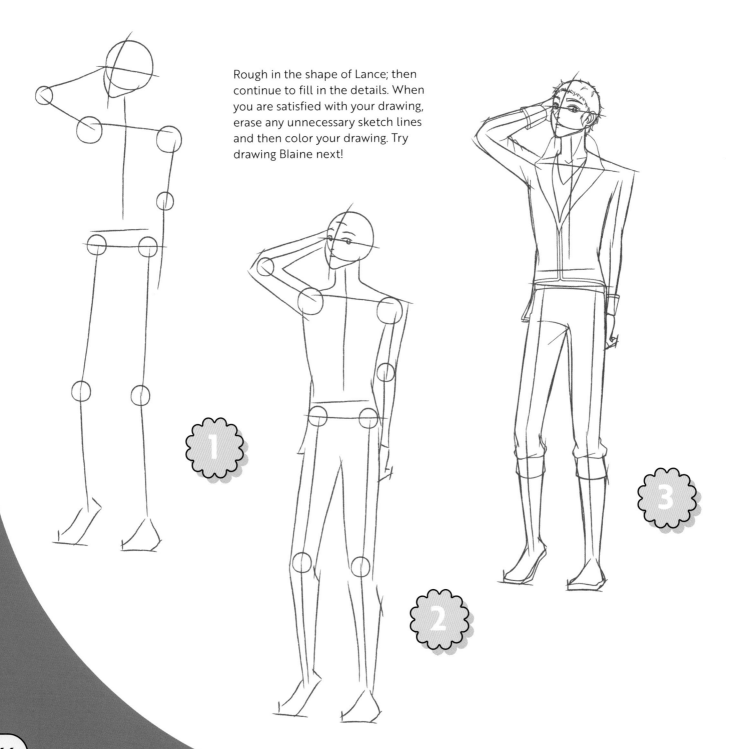

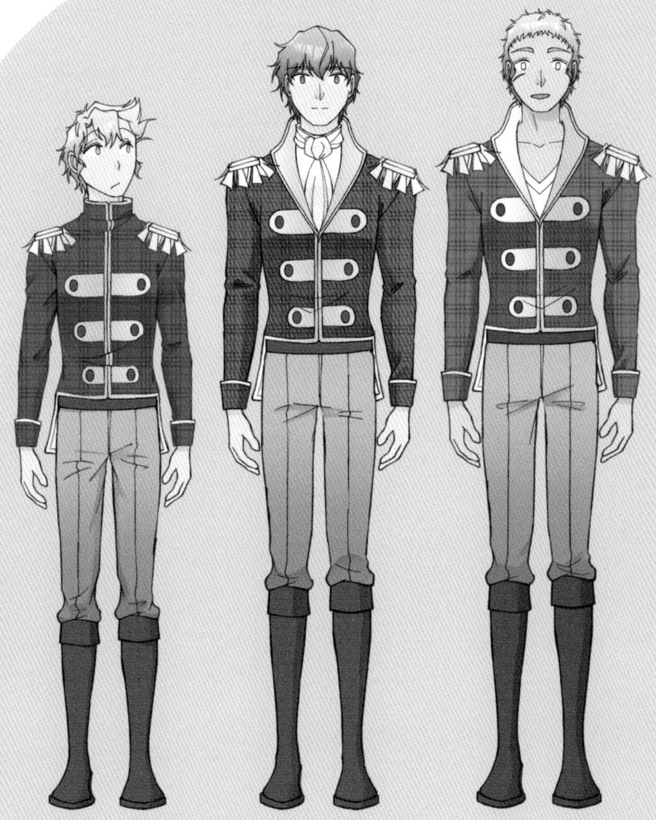

Lance is a tiny bit taller than Blaine, who is about a half head taller than Frederick. The brothers' clothes are nearly identical, as well.

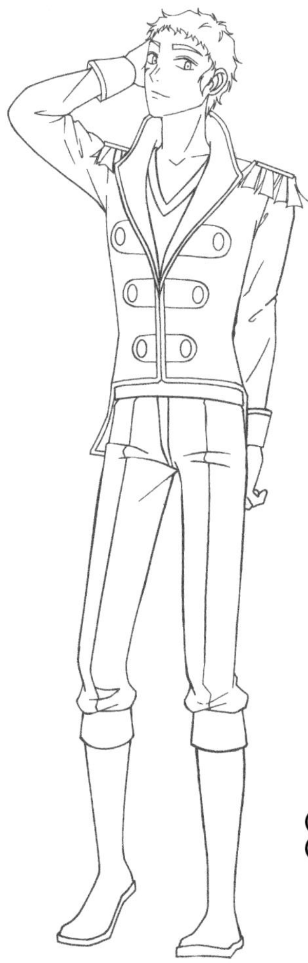

4

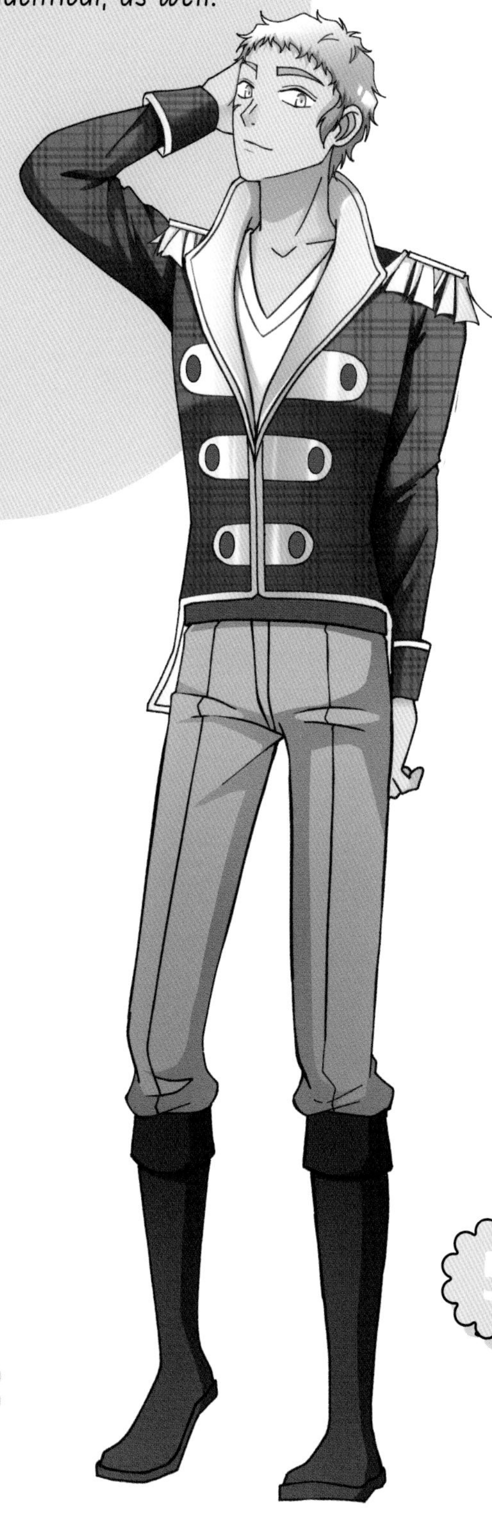

5

LEARN TO DRAW PREZ

Prez carries herself with confidence and authority, so her posture is generally tall and upright, with her shoulders back. She is friendly and therefore usually relaxed when she interacts with the other cursed princesses.

1

Start with a stick figure, marking the location of the hands, feet, and joints. Add guidelines to the face so you know where to place the features.

2

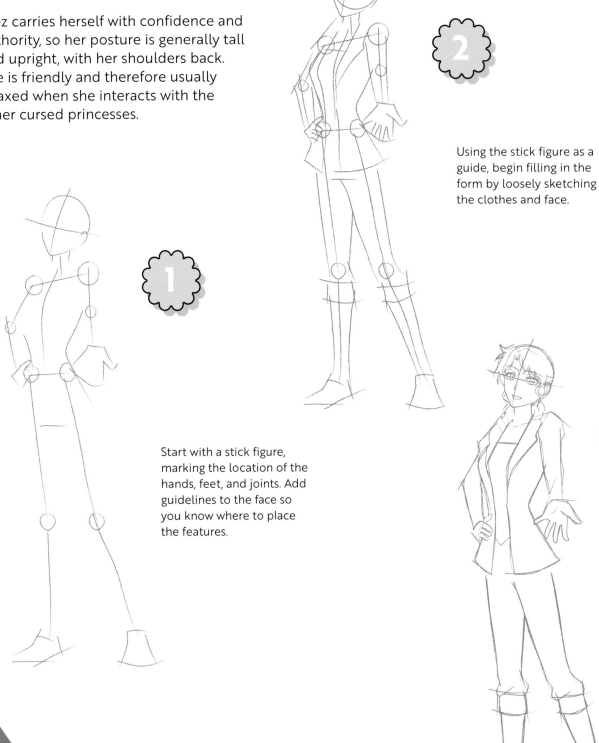

Using the stick figure as a guide, begin filling in the form by loosely sketching the clothes and face.

3

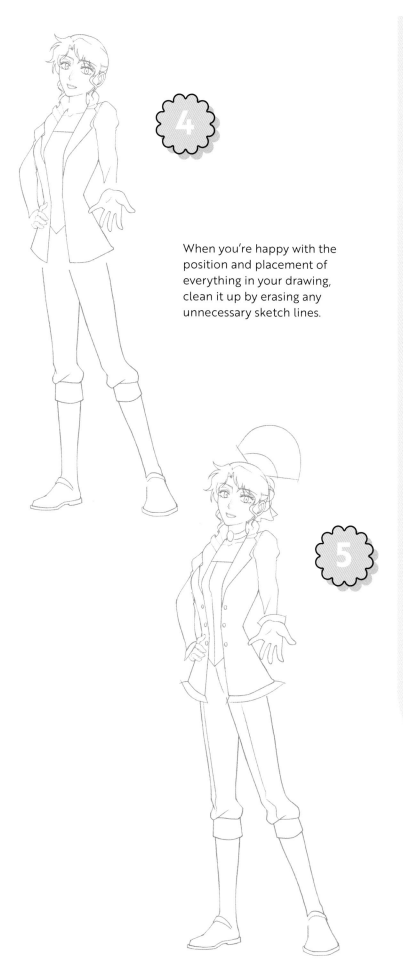

4

When you're happy with the position and placement of everything in your drawing, clean it up by erasing any unnecessary sketch lines.

5

Now it's time to jump into the details. Block in the general shapes of the headpiece and ruffles on the clothing. Add the vertical seams of her shirt and pants.

HEAD & CROWN

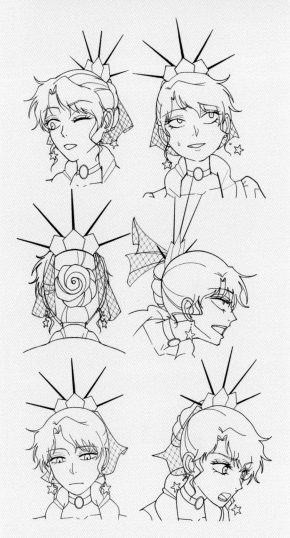

Notice how the position of Prez's headpiece changes with the position of her head. Her headpiece doubles as a weapon.

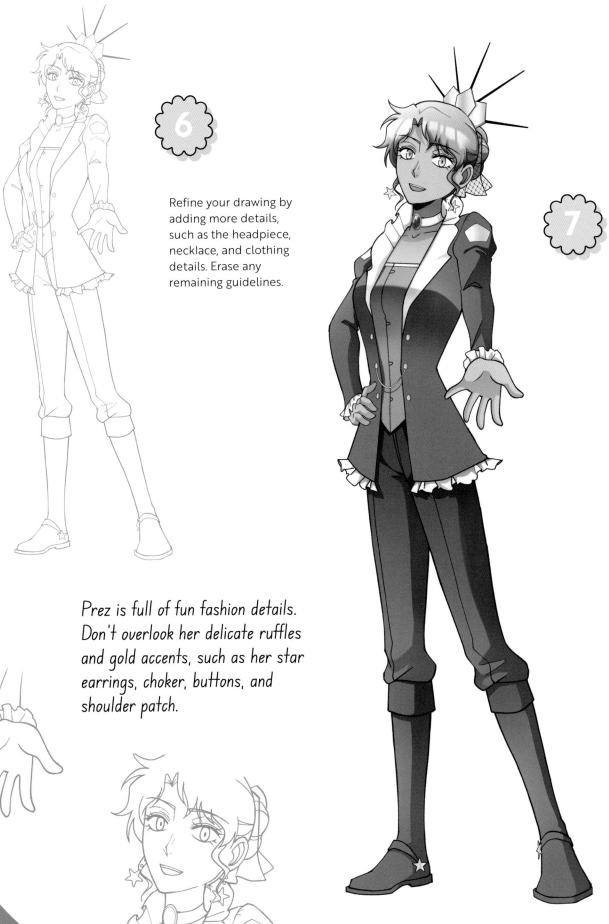

6

Refine your drawing by adding more details, such as the headpiece, necklace, and clothing details. Erase any remaining guidelines.

7

Color your drawing using the tools of your choice.

Prez is full of fun fashion details. Don't overlook her delicate ruffles and gold accents, such as her star earrings, choker, buttons, and shoulder patch.

LEARN TO DRAW THERMIDORA

Thermidora is part lobster with the claws to show for it, but she is otherwise hospitable. She has a curvy figure that is accentuated by her French-inspired fashion.

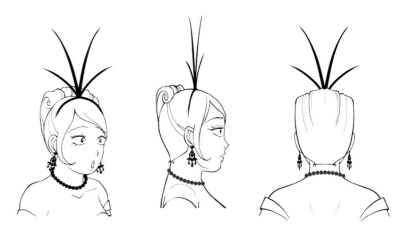

Thermidora's crown is made to look like lobster antennas. Her eyes are beady and black like a lobster's.

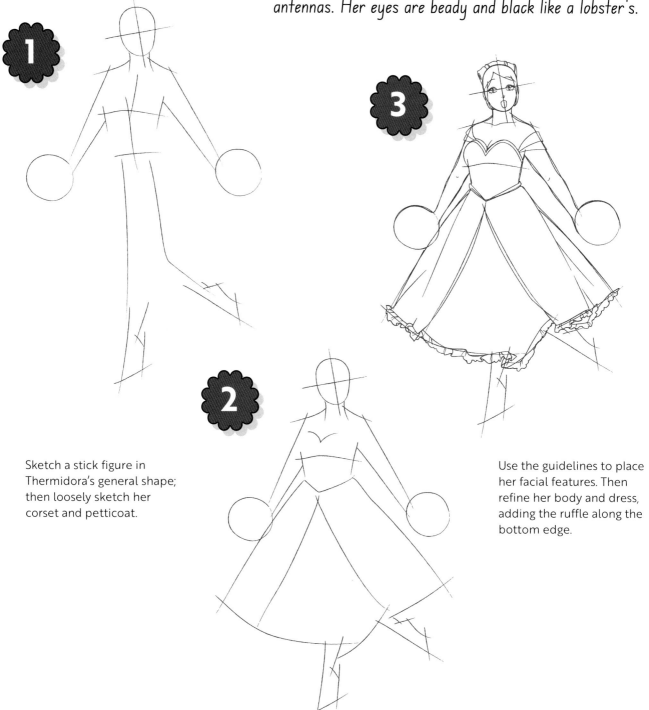

1 Sketch a stick figure in Thermidora's general shape; then loosely sketch her corset and petticoat.

2

3 Use the guidelines to place her facial features. Then refine her body and dress, adding the ruffle along the bottom edge.

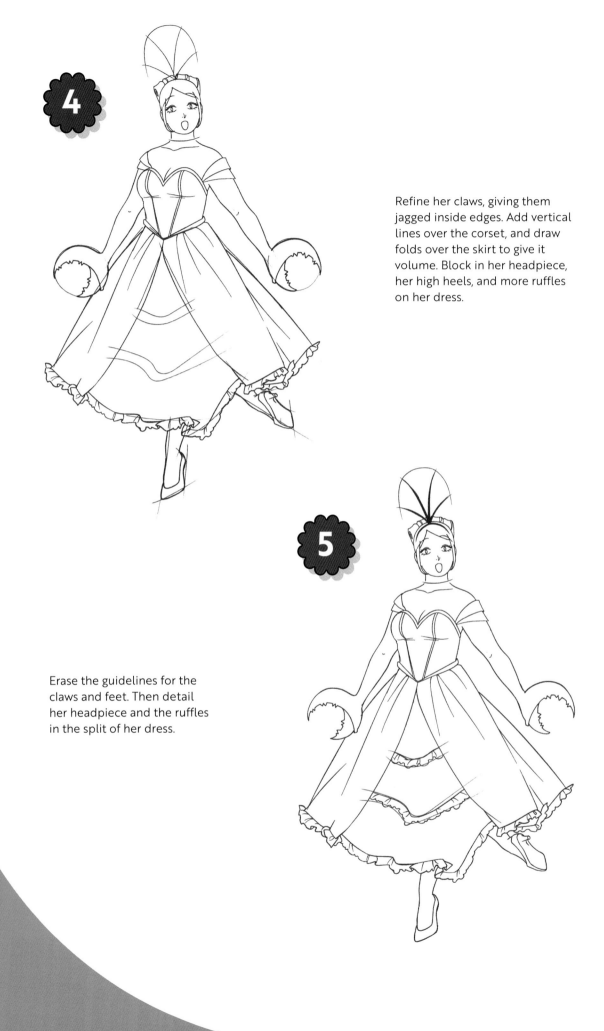

4

Refine her claws, giving them jagged inside edges. Add vertical lines over the corset, and draw folds over the skirt to give it volume. Block in her headpiece, her high heels, and more ruffles on her dress.

5

Erase the guidelines for the claws and feet. Then detail her headpiece and the ruffles in the split of her dress.

6

Give her just a few more elegant details, including a pearl necklace, chandelier earrings, and a shell brooch. Clean up your lines before adding color.

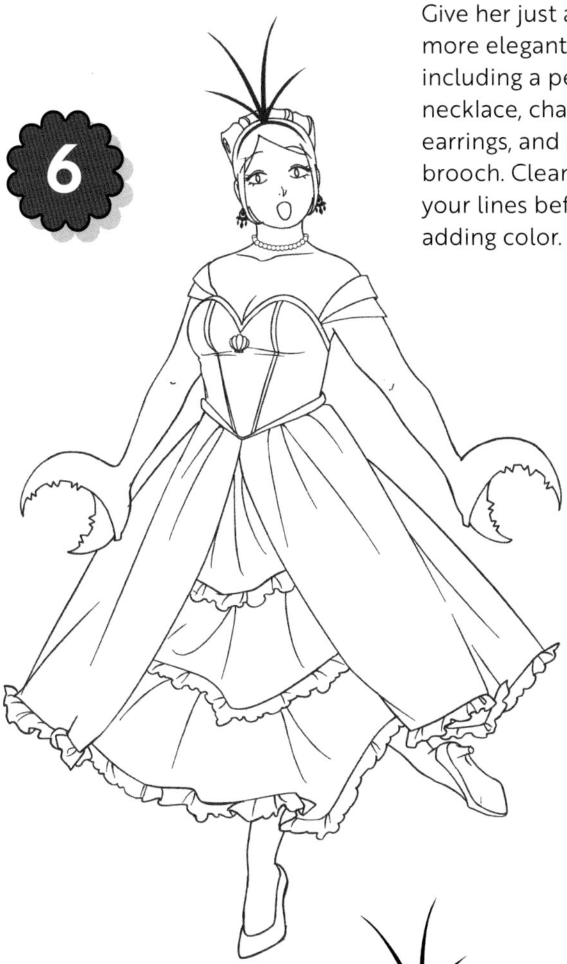

7

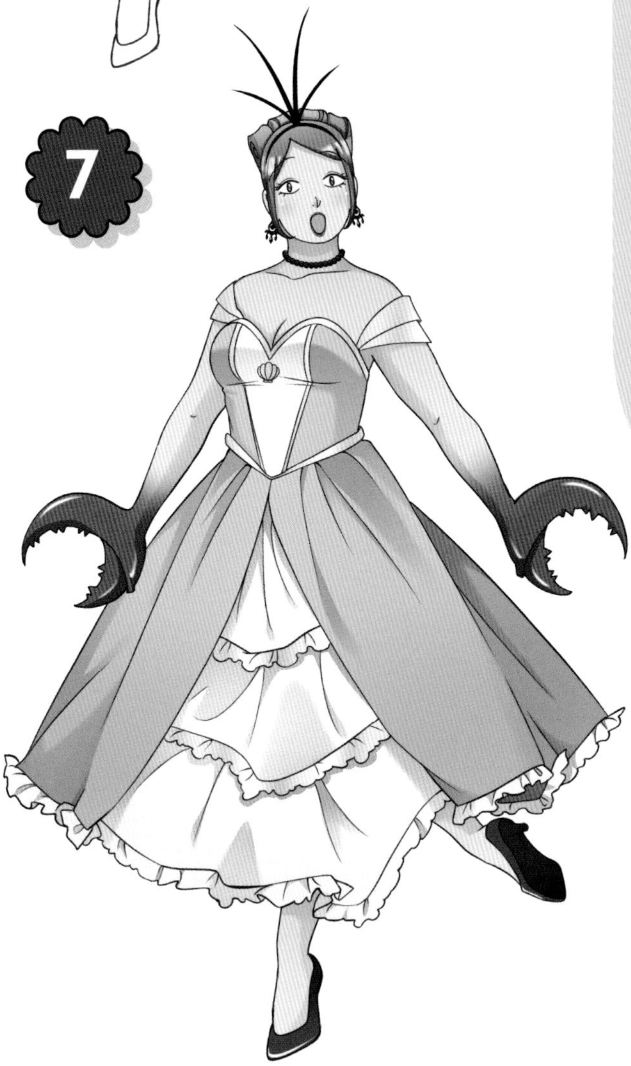

GOWN DETAILS

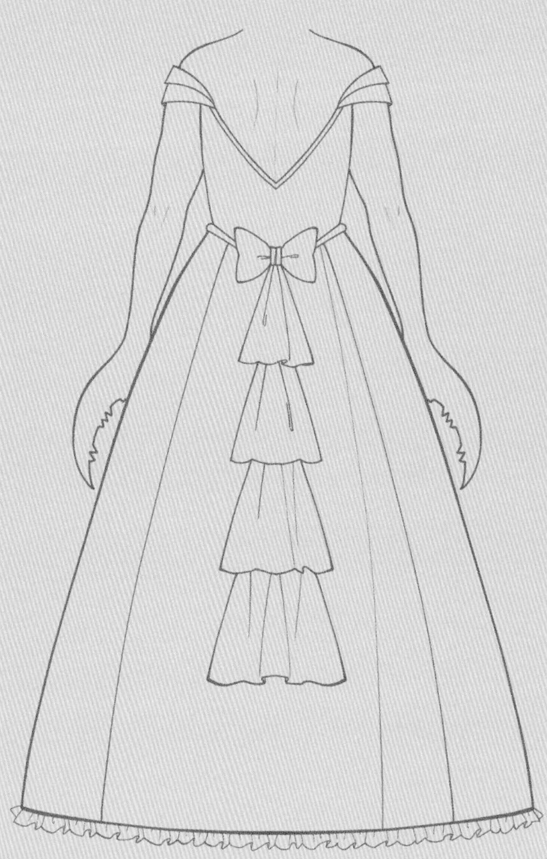

Thermidora wears a corset-type gown with a petticoat underneath and a ribbon sash that mimics a lobster tail.

LEARN TO DRAW SYRAH

Syrah would be a stereotypical beauty queen were it not for the fact that her nose grows when she tells a fib. She wears an off-the-shoulder dress with a long slit.

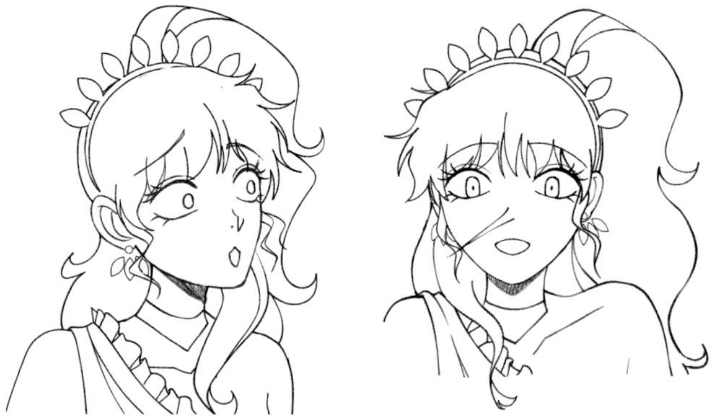

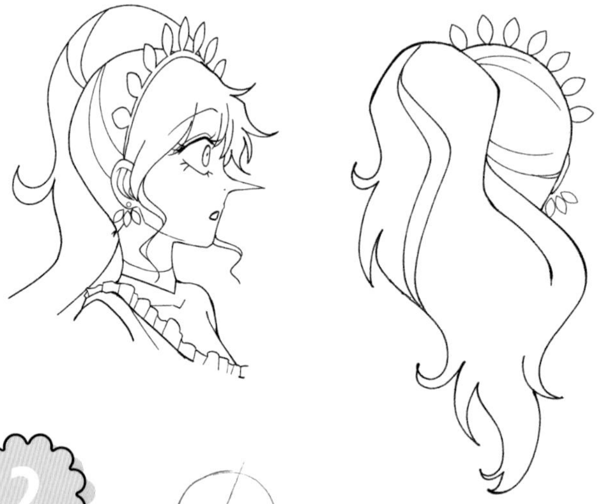

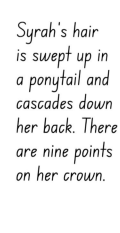

Syrah's hair is swept up in a ponytail and cascades down her back. There are nine points on her crown.

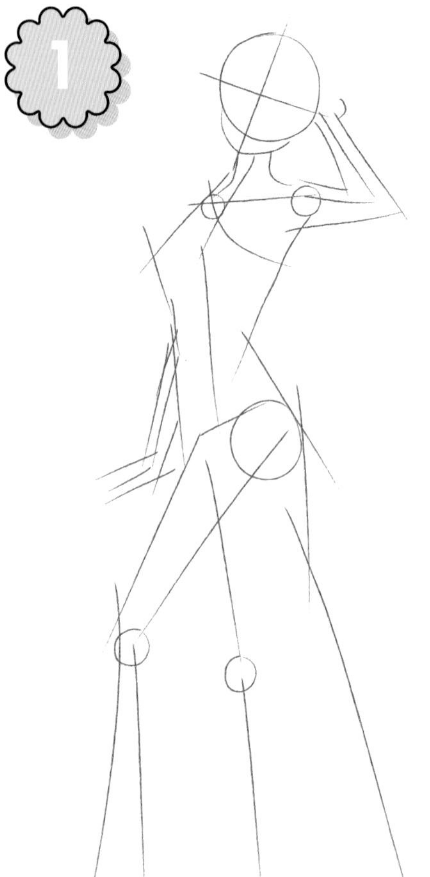
1

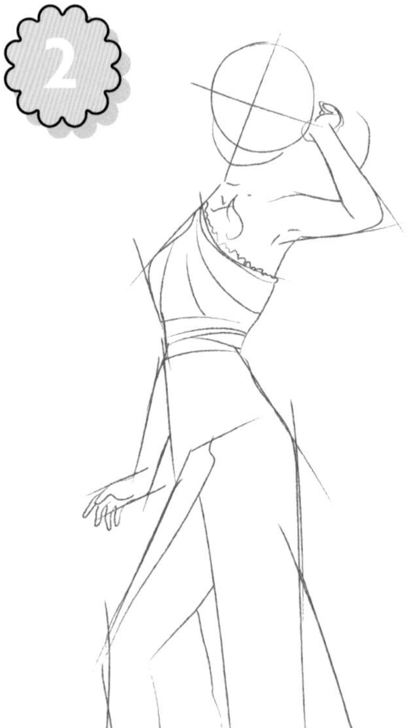
2

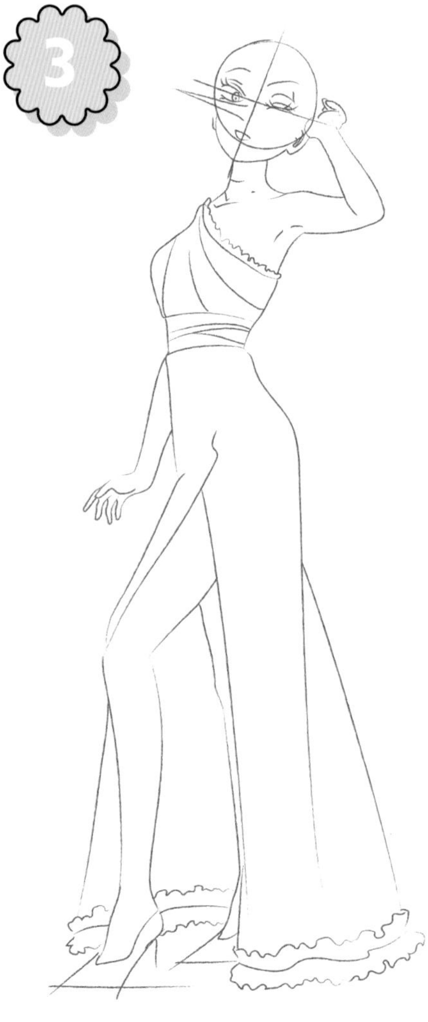
3

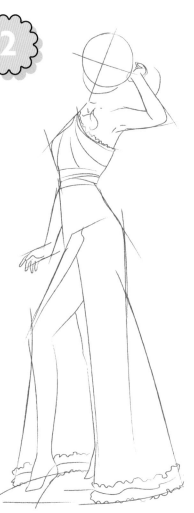

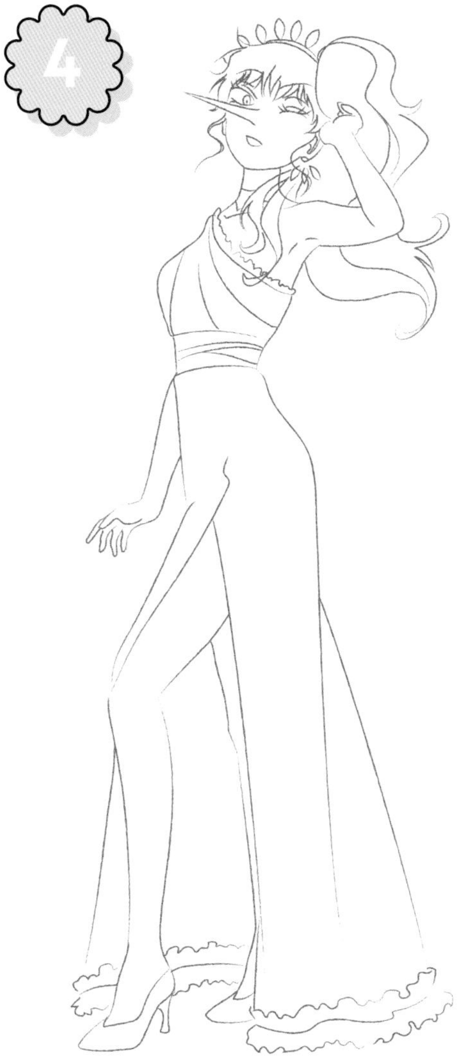
4

Using the stick figure as a guide, begin filling in the form by loosely sketching the clothes and face. When you're happy with your drawing, erase any unnecessary sketch lines. Then add color.

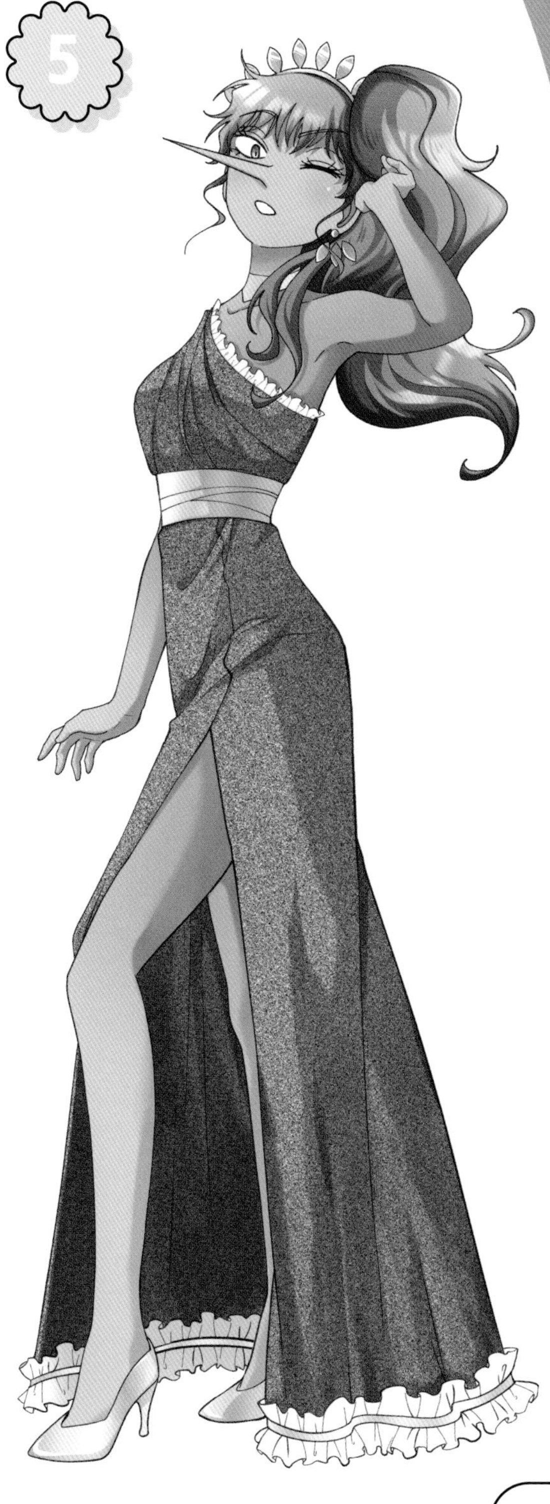
5

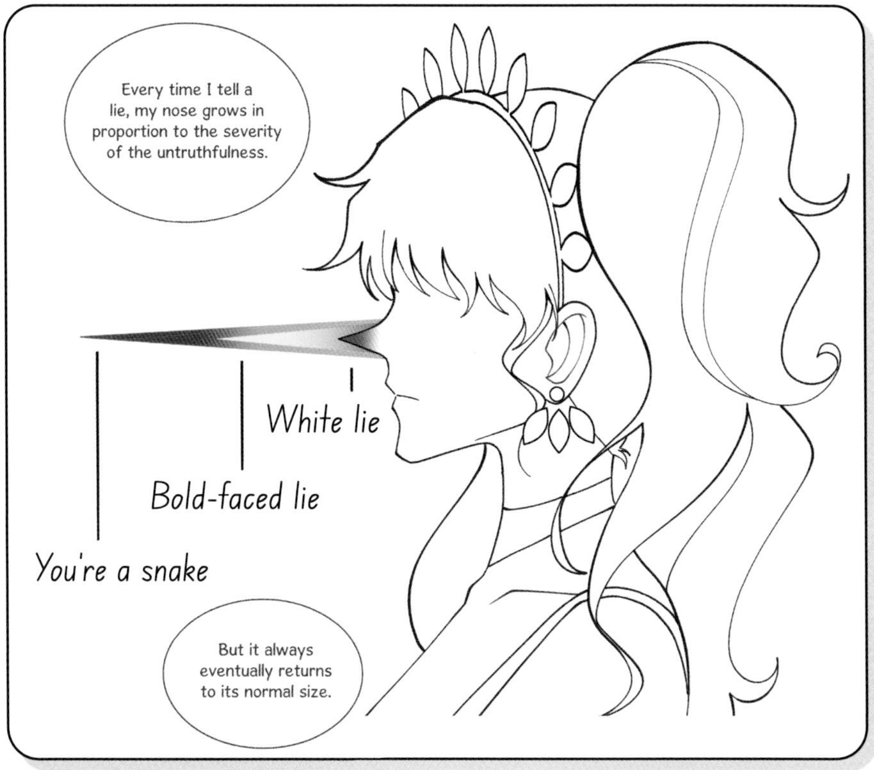
Every time I tell a lie, my nose grows in proportion to the severity of the untruthfulness.
White lie
Bold-faced lie
You're a snake
But it always eventually returns to its normal size.

LEARN TO DRAW MONIKA

Monika is cute and a little nervous—she never knows when she might change into a raven. She wears flowy robes and dresses that conceal her size.

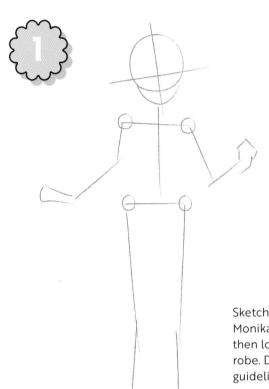

Monika is never without her glasses, which take up more space on her face than any of her features.

1

Sketch a stick figure in Monika's general shape; then loosely sketch the robe. Don't forget to add guidelines for the features.

2

3

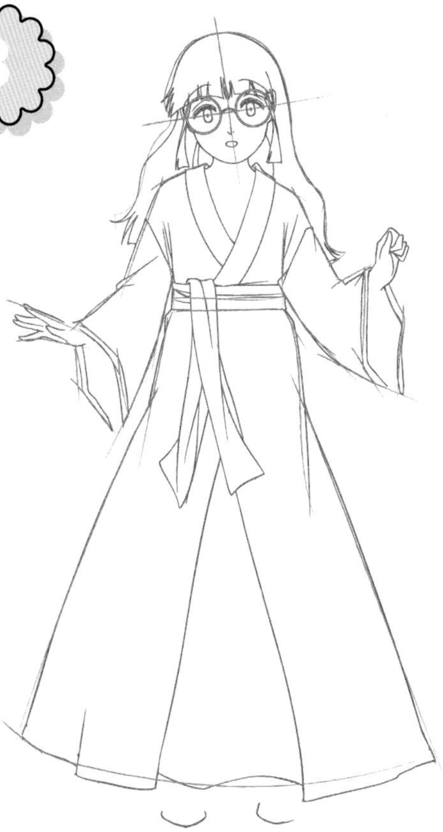

Continue to add the details and erase any unnecessary sketch lines as you go. When you've finished your drawing, add color.

4

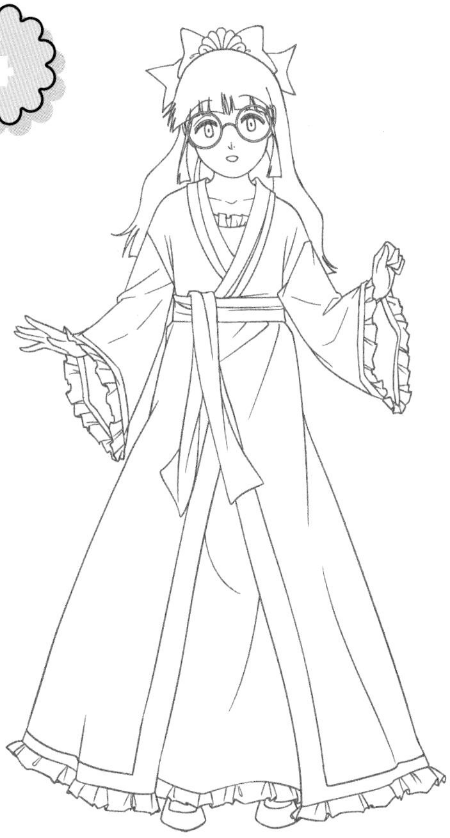

5

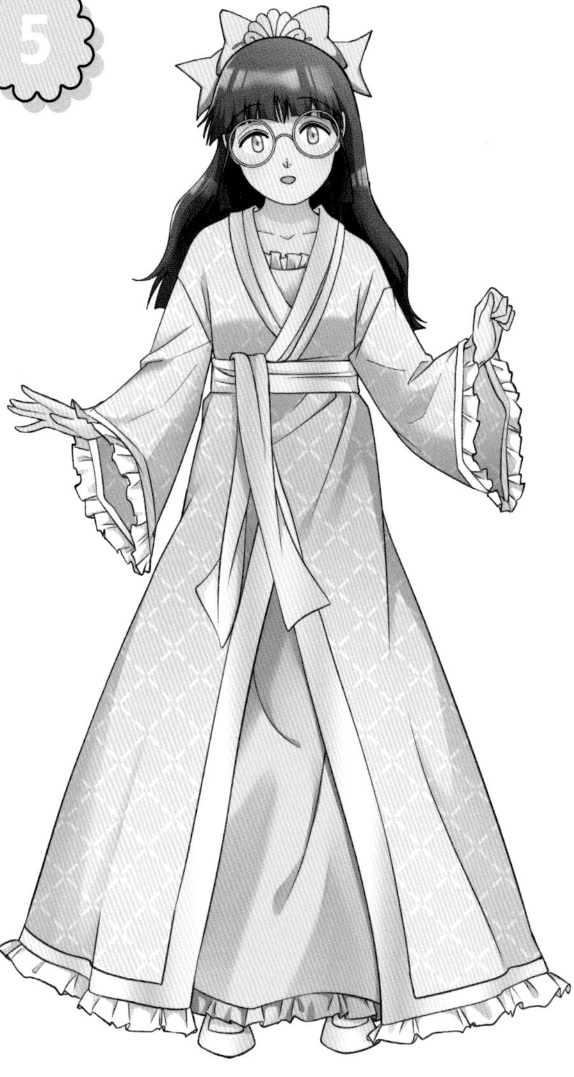

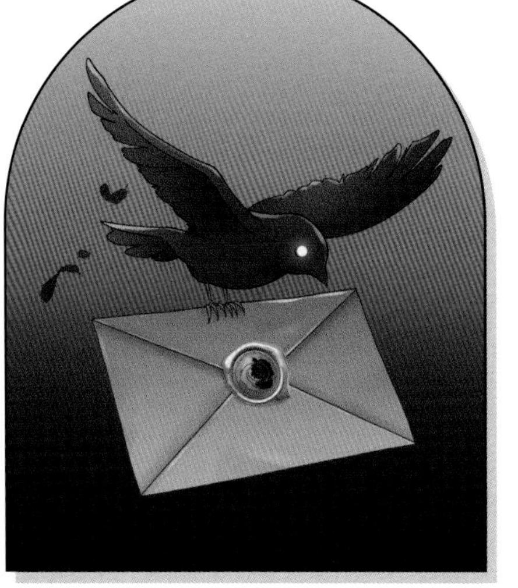

In bird form, Monika still manages to be helpful in delivering items and messages.

LEARN TO DRAW ABBI

Abbi may have the face of a senior citizen, but she's got the energy and sass of a teenager. To draw a body in motion, start with a stick figure as you would any other full-body pose.

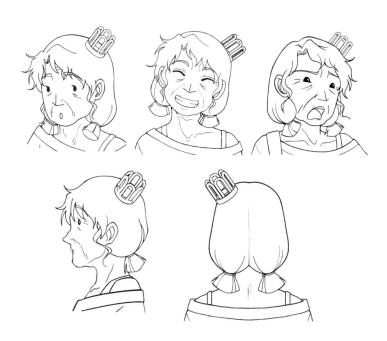

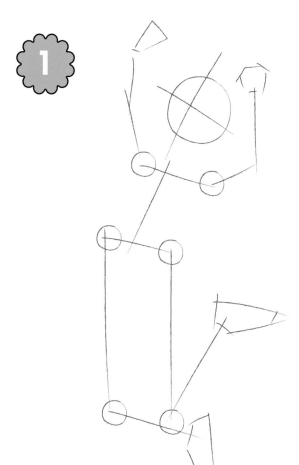

Abbi's appearance has a surprise element to it. From behind, her pigtails and tiara suggest she is a young teenage girl.

Rough in the form, maintaining the proportions of the body in size and shape.

3

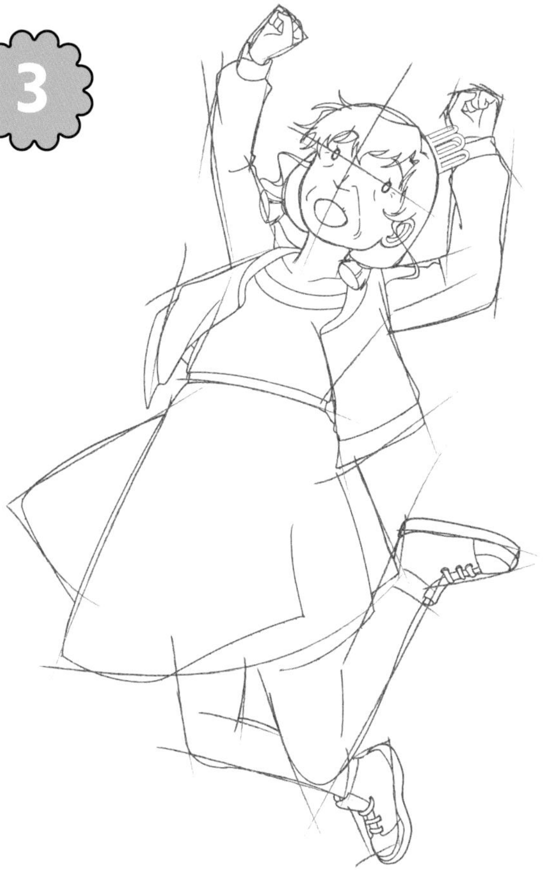

Begin adding the facial details and refining your sketch. Erase any old pencil marks or lines before going to color.

4

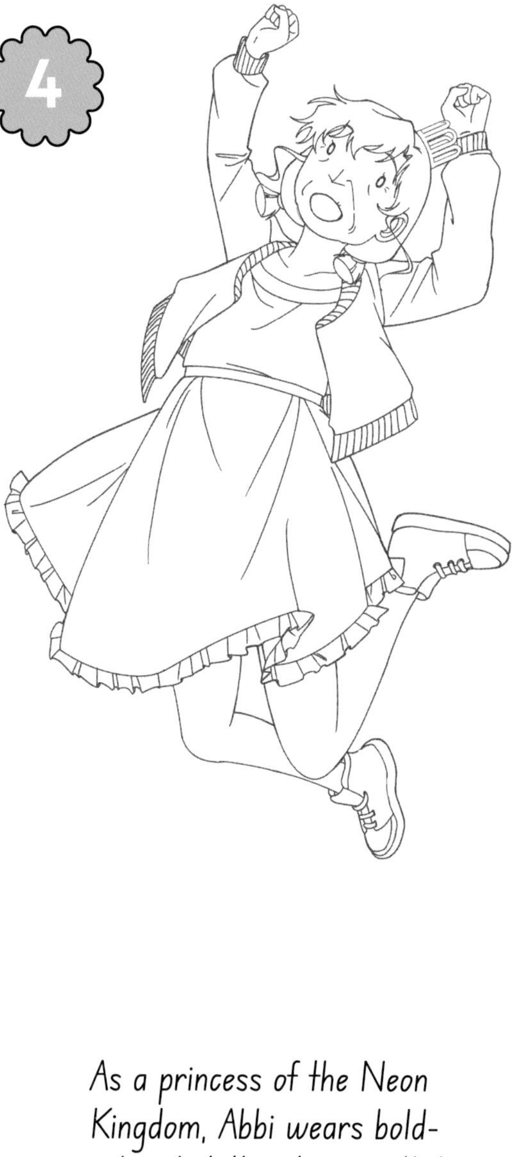

5

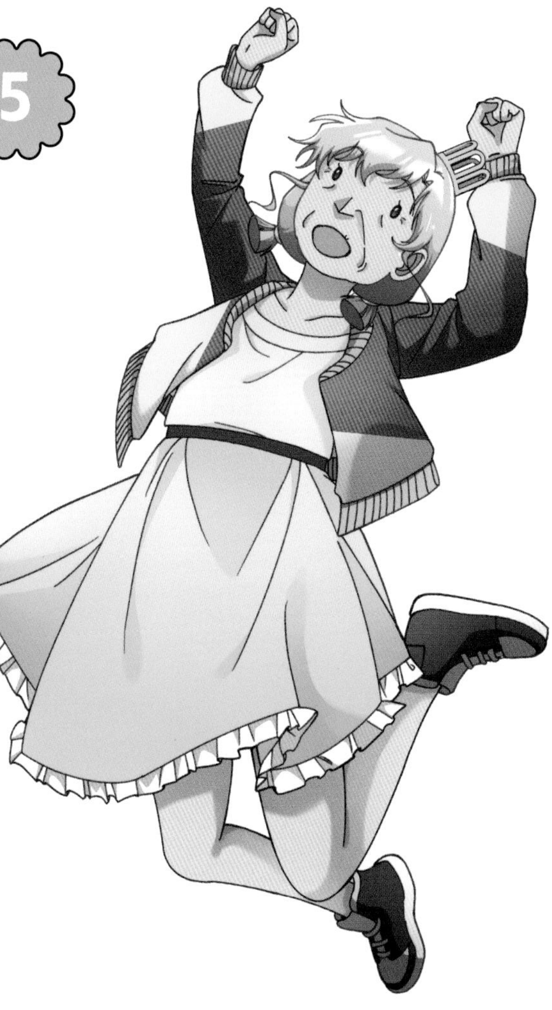

As a princess of the Neon Kingdom, Abbi wears bold-colored clothes to go with her vibrant turquoise-colored hair.

LEARN TO DRAW JOLIE

At first sight, Jolie presents as a stunning beauty. Once she removes her mask, however, her curse is revealed in the two gaping holes where her eyes should be.

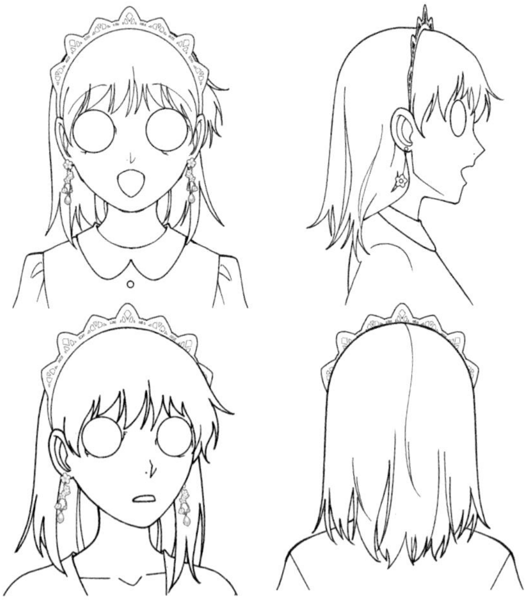

Jolie's real eyes are merely big, round saucers shaded in dark gray.

1

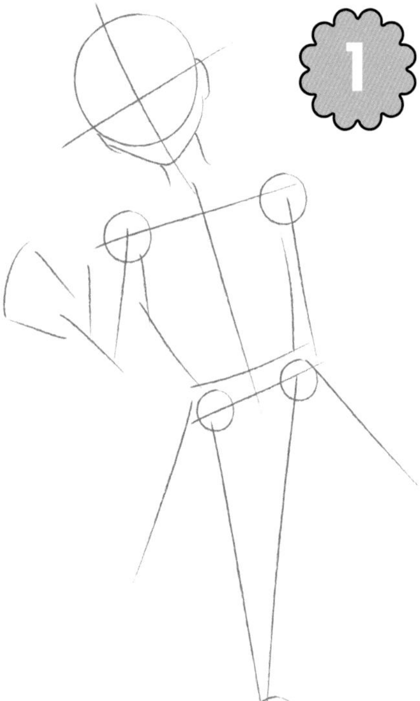

2

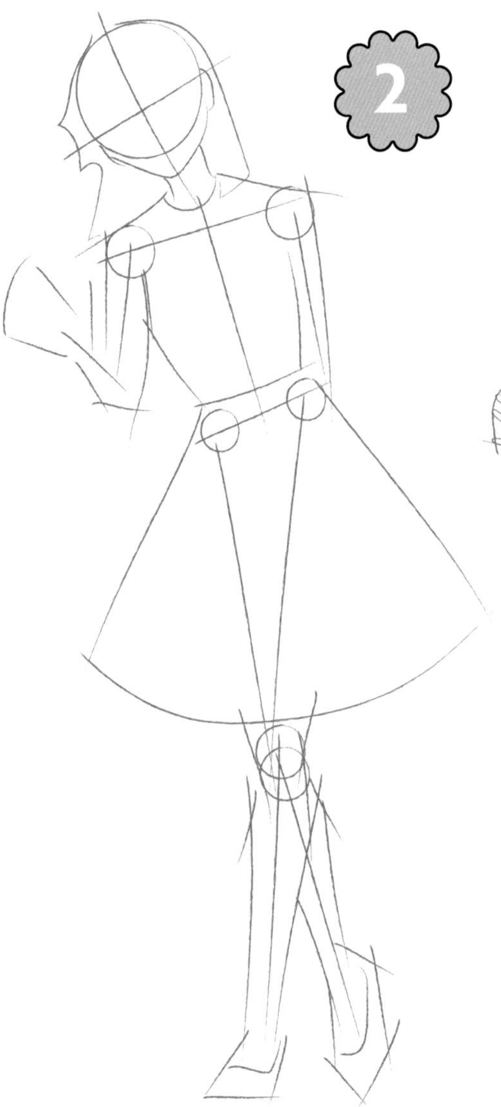

3

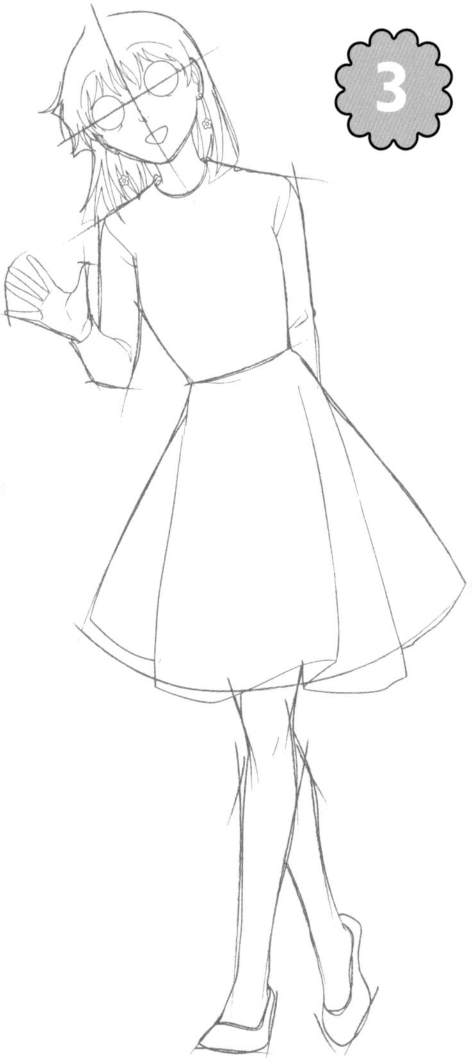

4

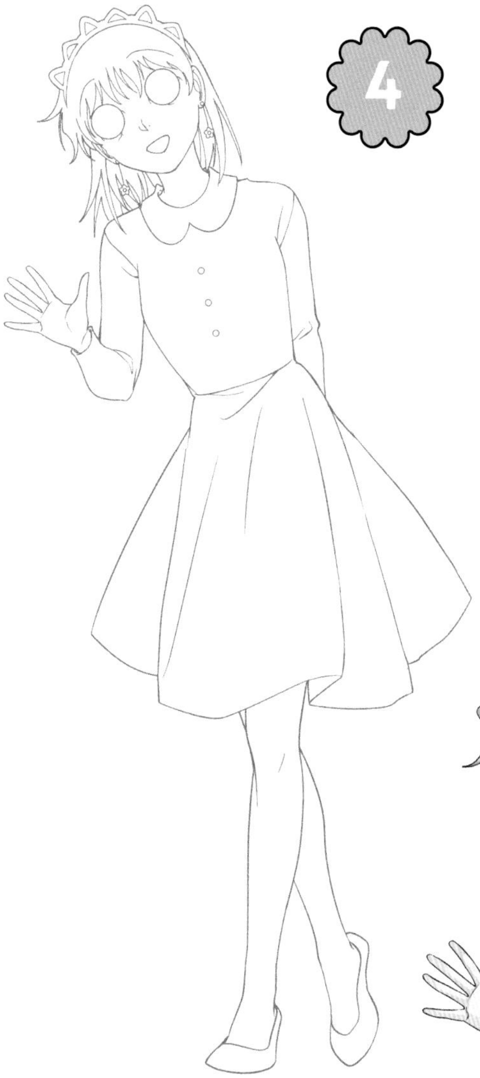

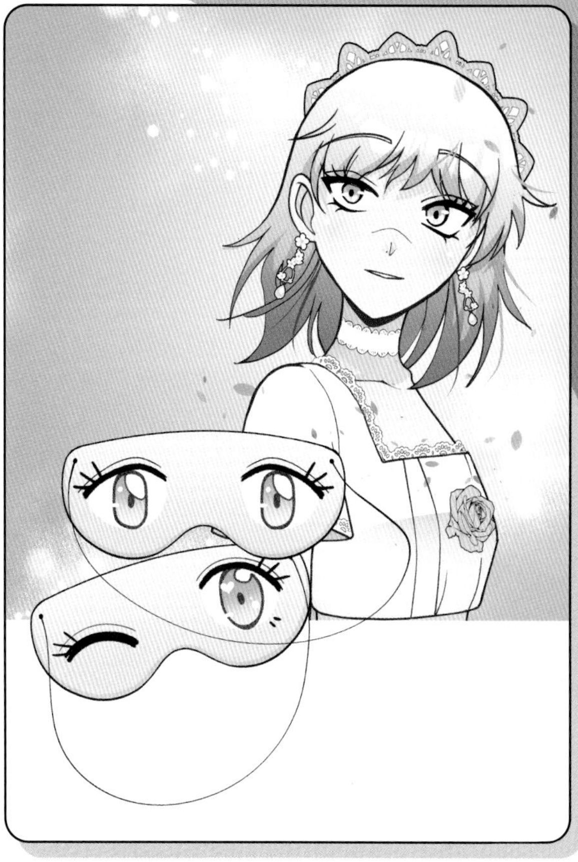

This cursed princess must wear different masks to express herself with her eyes!

5

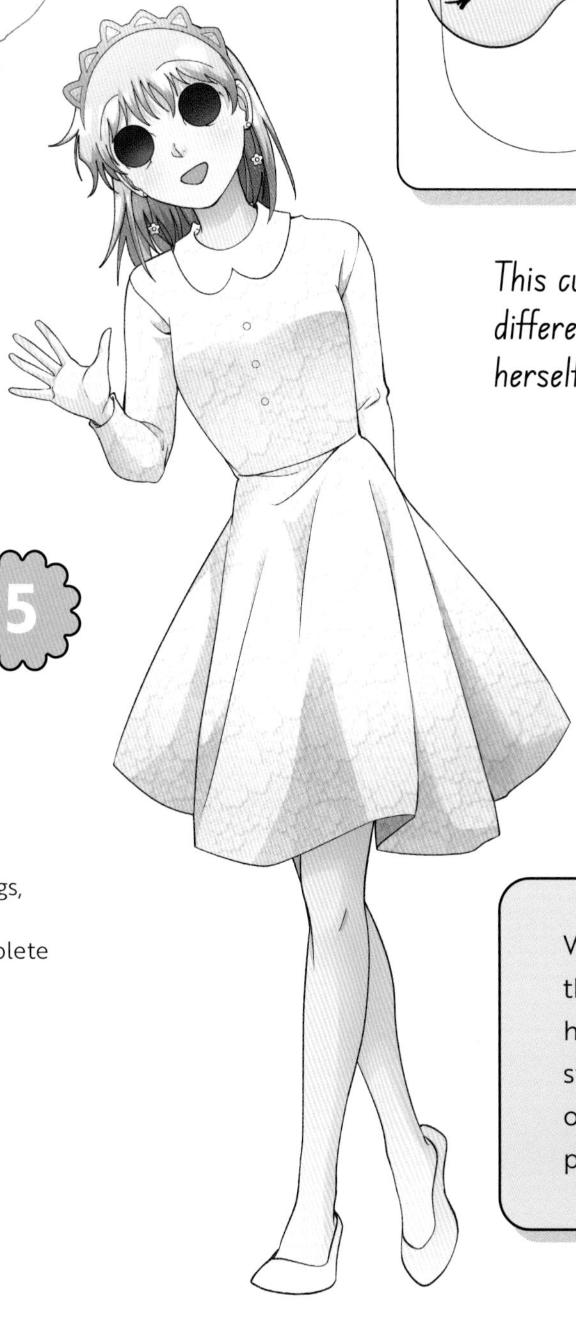

As with the other drawings, begin with a stick figure. Follow the steps to complete your drawing.

With the exception of the black holes that are her "real" eyes, Jolie's standard colors consist of soft, subtle shades of purple and white.

LEARN TO DRAW SAFFRON

Saffron has a tall athletic build—and one out-of-control hand that he covers with a glove. Practice drawing Saffron both with and without his protective hand covering.

Saffron is a little self-conscious about being a boy in the Cursed Princess Club. He also has an evil hand with a mind of its own, so his expressions can change rapidly depending on the action happening in the moment.

1

2

I guess I also have this evil hand that a goblin cast on me.
twitch
I can't control its movements and it terrorizes people around me. But it's really not that bad.

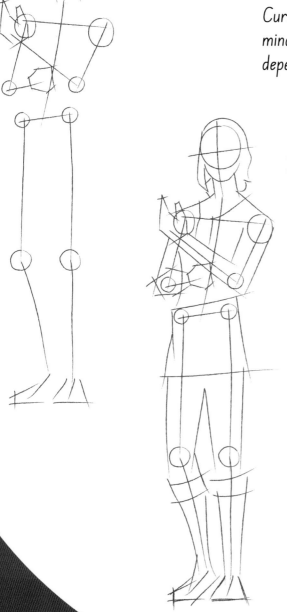

3

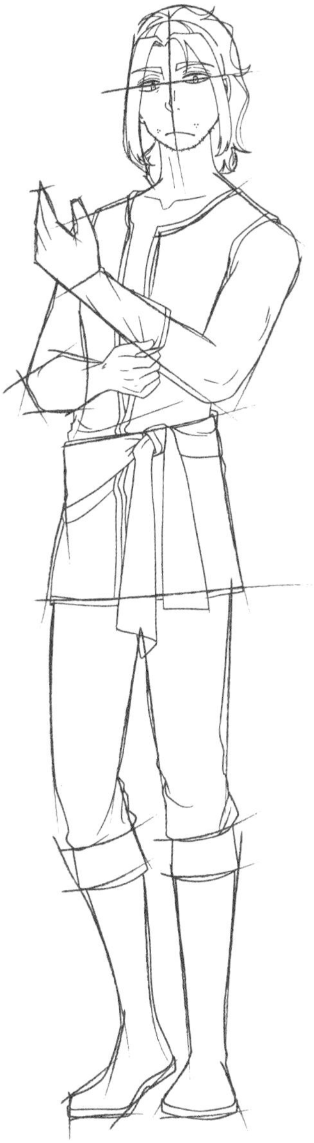

4

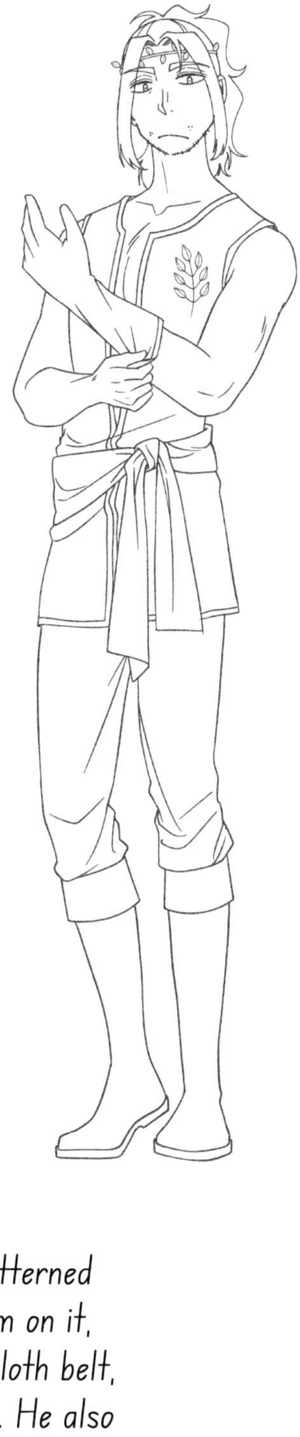

5

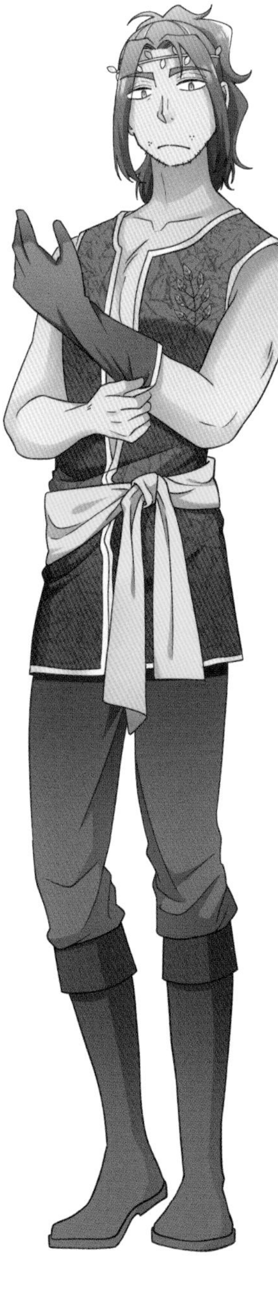

Saffron wears a patterned vest with an emblem on it, as well as a loose cloth belt, trousers, and boots. He also sports a thin headband.

LEARN TO DRAW WHITNEY

Whitney is tall and dreamy and can appear to have quite an intimidating aura at first. The intensity of his personality can be seen in his body posture, which is often tense.

Despite his intense outward appearance, Whitney is quite a stoic and a mentor in his reformed state.

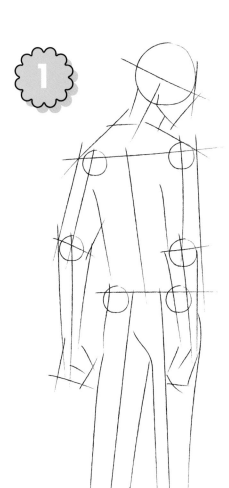

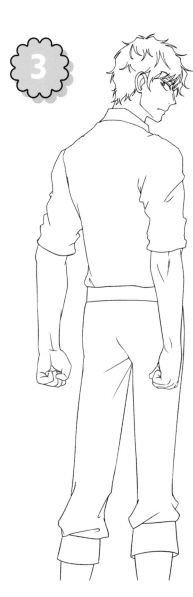

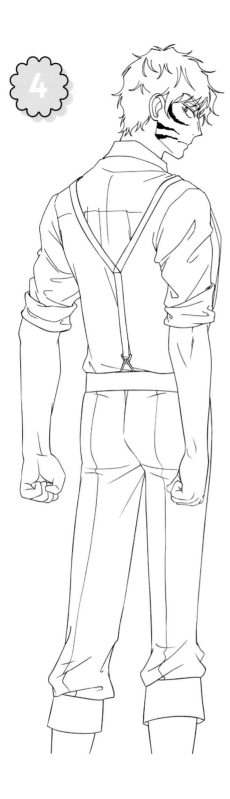

4

Start with a stick figure; then rough in the shape. Continue to follow the steps to finish the details and erase any unnecessary sketch lines. Then add color!

5

LEARN TO DRAW LAVERNE

Laverne is a sassy llama, who likes wearing jewelry, being pampered, and drinking wine. She wears lipstick and mascara and is loyal to King Leland as long as she gets what she wants. Nothing is too outrageous for Laverne's look.

1

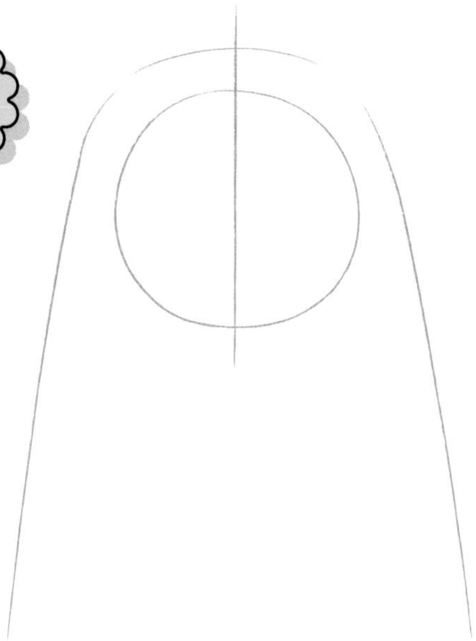

Rough out Laverne's basic shape and add the guidelines.

2

3

Draw her features on the guidelines; then begin polishing the details. When you are satisfied with your drawing, erase the sketch lines and add color.

4

5

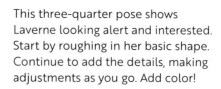

This three-quarter pose shows Laverne looking alert and interested. Start by roughing in her basic shape. Continue to add the details, making adjustments as you go. Add color!

Laverne is sometimes with a headscarf, sometimes with a bow, but she's always fabulous. She has a mole on left side of her mouth. She wears a pearl necklace with a heart locket and pearl bracelet on one of her wrists.

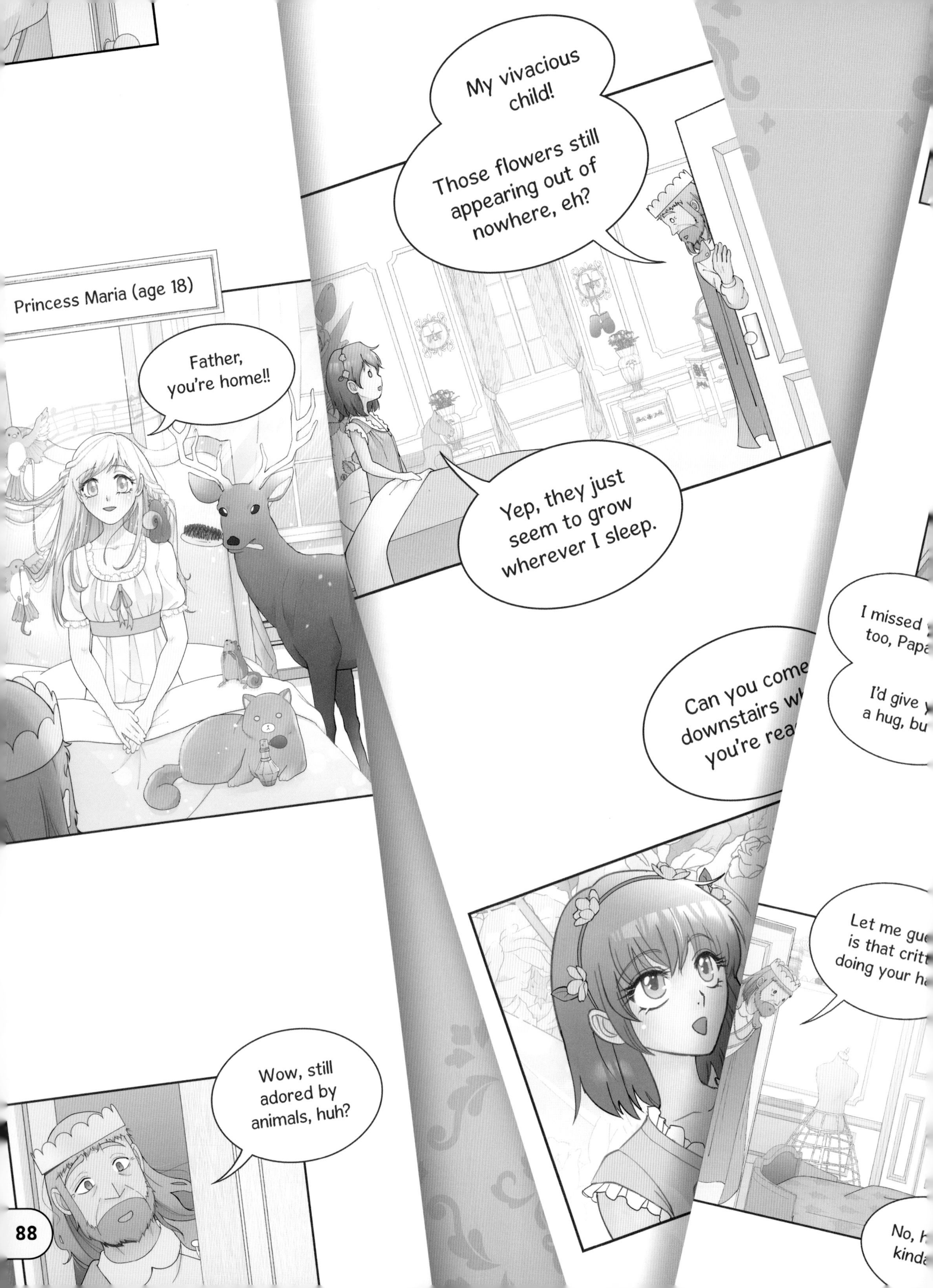

Princess Maria (age 18)
Father, you're home!!
Wow, still adored by animals, huh?
My vivacious child!
Those flowers still appearing out of nowhere, eh?
Yep, they just seem to grow wherever I sleep.
Can you come downstairs w
you're rea
I missed
too, Pap
I'd give
a hug, bu
Let me gu
is that crit
doing your h
No, h
kinda

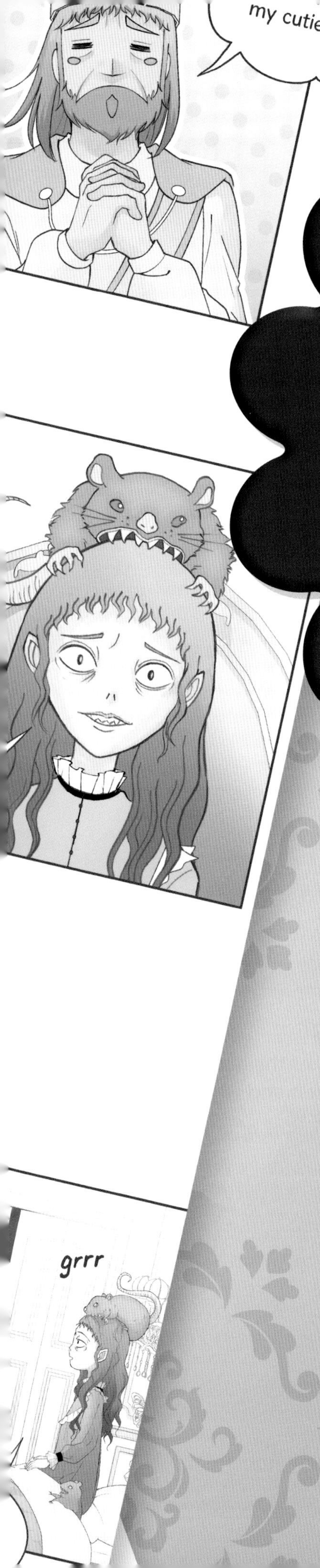
my cutie pie!!!
grrr

INTRODUCTION TO WEBTOONS

Turn your drawings into stories!

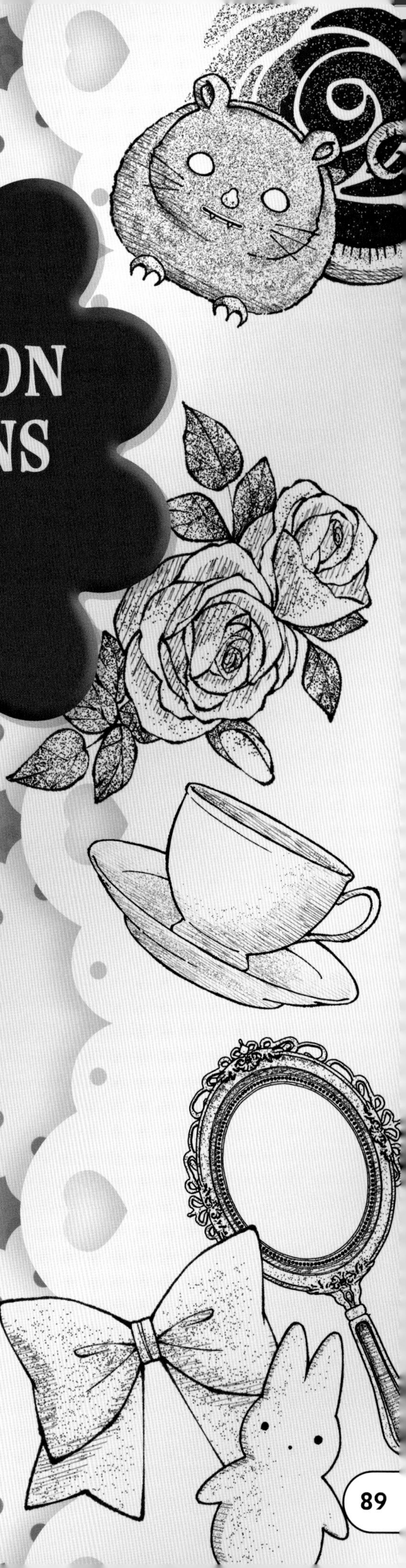

CHARACTER DEVELOPMENT

I wish I could say a lot of time and care goes into developing every character's design, but time is always tight in this industry! I start out writing concepts, personalities, and backgrounds for each character. From there, I loosely sketch each character once or twice. That is usually all I have time for before drawing them in the comic. I often go back and change things after I have more time to sit with them.

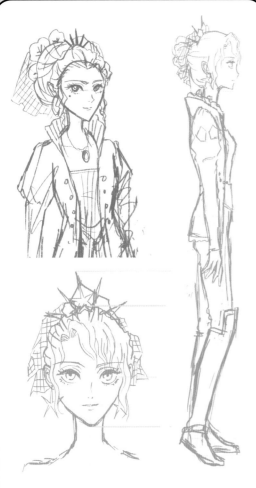

Prez was designed to embody strength, resiliency, and leadership, while also exploring the trappings of these usually positive traits as well. Her outfit is loosely inspired by Disney's Snow White but was turned into a Princess Charming pantsuit.

Her headband doubles as a weapon.

She has star-shaped buckles on the inside of her boots.

I started out wanting this story to have a soft, pastel, retro, shoujo anime feeling to it, combined with classic fairy-tale/storybook tropes. I was inspired by anime like Sailor Moon, Cardcaptor Sakura, and *Revolutionary Girl Utena*, but I also wanted to have features of Gwendolyn and other members of the Cursed Princess Club very much juxtapose that.

Maria's design centered around a hairstyle that her birds would braid for her every morning. After trying a few variations, I settled on long golden hair with two braided buns and ribbons.

Because Lorena has flowers bloom around her, I tried several ideas of flowers, leaves, and branches adorning her head. In the end, I settled for a pink flower headband.

The Pastel King is the epitome of an over-protective, loving father. Behind his bumbling countenance and limp gray hair lies a fiery rage toward anyone or anything that might come after his daughters. I wanted a cute Peter Pan collar for the King's uniform and all Pastel service uniforms.

Monika was named after a character in the visual novel *Doki Doki Literature Club!*, which definitely inspired me in terms of taking a cute, silly premise for a story and having the tone shift and disintegrate over time.

COMPLETING A SCENE

Here is an example of what it's like for me and my art team to take a sketch to a finished illustration. This was a spooky piece made for a banner on the WEBTOON front page to celebrate Halloween.

SKETCHES

Think about the dimensions of the art you need to make and how your characters will fill that space. Create a loose sketch of the characters.

Next, it's time to create the line art. If you are drawing digitally, turn the opacity of your sketch down until it is lightly visible. Then make a new layer and trace everything with a pen of your choice.

Color everything in with flat colors. When doing this digitally, I like to create a separate layer to color each element, as this allows me to easily change, test, and play around with lots of colors!

Add shading based on the direction of the light source. In this example, the light is coming from the two candles on either side of Gwen and Frederick. For many panels of my webcomic, this where the illustration would be complete.

Adding lighting to your illustration is great for setting a specific mood. By casting a translucent black layer over everything and then adding neon green highlights, the illustration becomes much spookier.

ABOUT THE CREATOR

Lambcat is a small, omnivorous, and easily frightened creature who has burrowed deep into the Pacific Northwest to draw comics and make music, and can be lured out by Bill Evans records and anything birthday-cake flavored.

I would love for you to share your drawings! Feel free to tag me on Instagram and Twitter: @iamlambcat